DESTINY

Shilo Manor, book three

by

Charlene A. Wilson

Shilo Manor series~Destiny

What Readers are Saying

"Charlene Wilson has done it again! Just when you think Cole and Anna/Mianna have had their happy ending, Wilson twists the knife in another direction. The Gods of Meridian are calling their sons back and the Shilo brothers must say goodbye to Cornerstone Deep – but this is not the end; it's only the beginning! Whimsical magic, true love, and family secrets abound in the [Shilo Manor] series, and book three, Destiny, is no exception." —*Author J.D. Brown*

"Destiny: [Shilo Manor], Book 3 by Charlene A. Wilson was definitely great. I sat down and read it in one day because I was absolutely entranced by each of the characters. I loved that the reader was able to really get involved in everything that was happening, and that you could see things from each character's point of view to really get into the story. There's a lot of action going on, but you can tell that all of the characters love one another and that the family bond is stronger than anything else.

... Destiny by Charlene A. Wilson is definitely not one to miss." — *Samantha, Readers' Favorite*

"Destiny is a stunningly beautiful commencement to this marvelous series that brings with it a sense of true fulfillment and an ever-present promise of more. Charlene A Wilson is a truly remarkable author who knows how to touch your very soul before you even realize it yourself. She will reach into your heart and make you feel every word and emotion with more intensity and longing than you ever thought possible. If you want a story that will rearrange your heart and challenge you in every way, then this series is the perfect opportunity to discover and experience a new author that is full of surprises and will delight all of your senses." —*Amazon Customer*

Charlene A. Wilson

Destiny Copyright © 2018 by Charlene A. Wilson

Published by
Spectrum Publishing
Morrilton, Arkansas 72110

ISBN-10: 0989984656
ISBN-13: 978-0-9899846-5-2

Credits
Editor: Susan Davis
Cover: Magicgrafix
Special thanks to the Cover Models.

DESTINY

by

Charlene A. Wilson

Table of Contents

Shilo Manor series~Destiny

Note from the Author

Hello loves,

I'm delighted you chose to read book three, *Destiny*! The books in the Shilo Manor series are best read in order to grasp the full story.

The first few books in this series were created from a dream and are littered with scenes from that dream. Actually, it was a nightmare! But all through the frightening things that happened, dreamer's omniscience allowed me to know the strange men ... their pasts, their dreams, and I knew they saw life with an eternal perspective. Experiences, including mistakes, during your life cause growth, and growth leads to understanding. Their soul mates last forever, whatever the state of their current lifetime!

I hope you fall in love with them as much as I have.

May your dreams be magical,
Charlene A. Wilson

Dedication

To my wonderful son, Thomas.

He's patient with this air-headed mom of his and has been my rock through many hard times. I love you, Sweetheart. Happy birthday!

Chapter One

Stars blinked, and Vincent scowled at the firmament. They mocked him—tiny gems as out of his reach as the treasure he sought. With a snarl, he scanned the area around the empty town square, whirled to face Simpson drive, and then jabbed his hand toward the deserted street of the city's east side.

"Orvertre!"

The summoning command echoed through the night and then ebbed into the quiet atmosphere with no result.

A frog croaked from Center Creek somewhere within the park to his right. The urban green rustled, and deep shadows waved as the breeze whispered along the tall border hedges. A cat padded from an alley between the north side commerce onto the sidewalk and then looked his way. The dim streetlight reflected in its eyes, two silver discs that taunted alongside the night sky.

With a growl, he punched his frustration into the air. Blue neon flashed from his fist. The bolt highlighted the crimson brick storefronts and plowed into the street with a resounding blast. Asphalt bulleted the commerce, shattering glass behind the barred windows, and pelted the granite griffin perched on top of the corner archway of the entrance to Shilo Park.

The cat darted back the way it came.

Vincent snarled. Turning toward the city center, he clenched his jaw and glared around the empty court. How many times had he tried to summon the Mother Earth beads here already? Every faithful follower of the gods had come to witness the absence of Gryffin. When they finally left, the park was in shambles. It took three weeks to pick up all the rubble and return the vegetation to its rightful state.

He glanced over his shoulder at the stone gargoyle. The god of conformance couldn't have made a more striking statement with his disappearance—and the beads couldn't have been lost at a worst time. *Anyone could have stashed them away, thrilled to find such a keep.*

Vincent ground his teeth together so hard his temples ached. Humidity thickened the early summer night and carried the sulfuric odor from the west side industries. It coated his senses with added irritation. Where was the floral scent of Shilo Park? He needed the comfort it held.

Releasing his breath, he whispered a vow he didn't intend to sustain. "Elaina, you will never touch another magical charm as long as you live."

He glanced at his watch and sighed an anxious breath. *I need to get home.*

How long before his brothers questioned his excursions? How long could he keep the disappearance of the relic a secret?

Furling his cape, he dispersed his elements into a fine mist. He allowed his dark essence to meander as he flew the length of the boulevard, recalling the crowded scene. Pilgrimage buggies, tents, covered wagons; they were only a portion of the massive gathering of faithful that had finally cleared the area.

Irritation rippled his essence. With a growl, he conceded failure and headed over the southern apricot orchards to Shilo Manor.

Chapter Two

Elaina wrapped her hands around her coffee mug and grinned. Vanilla wafted from the wide kitchen island as her twin nieces, Mandy and Mechenzie, baked with James and her sister, Linda. The cause of the aroma became clear as Linda tipped a bottle of flavoring upright next to Mandy and then dabbed at the ingredient with a towel.

As Elaina leaned her head to the side, she couldn't help but consider James' acceptance of her sister and a set of rambunctious six-year-olds. His elation at stepping into the role of Daddy—albeit through socialized adoption—brought the Sentinel family a new perspective of life, to say the least. She saw it in every correspondence James had with the girls. Cole's demeanor had even softened, though the return of his reincarnated love could have something to do with that. She glanced to her side where Anna sat gazing at her wedding rings. *And they couldn't make a better couple.*

But Vincent... His eyes sparkled brighter, the color of his lips deepened, and Gods help her, if there was a way to be the one to bring him a child of his own to increase that reaction, she would find it.

James' countenance glowed as he waved a finger and more towels flew from the pantry and then landed neatly beside them. The knob on the black lacquered stove clicked to preheat, and she realized the motion had a dual purpose.

Mechenzie dumped flour into a large bowl, and Mandy immediately shoved her hands into the powder, wiggling her fingers.

"It's odd to see them baking instead of you." Anna chortled as she leaned toward Elaina.

Jarred from her thoughts, Elaina managed to keep her palms on her cup.

Anna scooted closer on the bench of the breakfast nook. Her bowtie lips curled upward. "Just look at them. A perfect little family."

Relaxing, Elaina sighed and let her shoulders sag. Her children would crack the eggs too hard, shake the canister too vigorously, and dump ingredients over the measuring cups. There would be two—a boy and a girl, Vincent Jr. and Lacey. They'd have Vincent's dark eyes, jet-black hair, and stunning smile. There wouldn't be a speck of her strawberry blonde between them. They would...

Cole's shuffling steps entered the kitchen and then paused behind her as he leaned in close and whispered in her ear. "Yes. It will be perfect. Complete with an intolerance to cooperate that will end in baking the eggs before they can be beaten."

Elaina looked up at him. At times like these, the skills the Shilo brothers held only managed to embarrass her. *Tell me he didn't read my thoughts.*

He nodded with a grin, and his midnight eyes sparkled with mirth. "And the cinnamon will make the youngest sneeze, causing sparks to smash the glass bowls and melt the butter." He chuckled and cocked his head with a squelch on his cheek. "What a waste of butter."

Linda laughed and looked at them, traces of flour patted on her cheek. "Are you dreaming again, little sister?"

James steadied Mandy's hand as she poured the vanilla into the mix. "Cole has no business viewing your thoughts, no matter the subject, Elaina."

Cole shook his head as he took a seat beside Anna. "I wasn't reading her thoughts. It's not hard to come to the conclusion on my own. It's all she talks about."

Elaina peeked at him from the corner of her eyes as he settled next to Anna, set his coffee mug on the breakfast nook table, and then wrapped an arm around his love. His lips pressed to her dark locks.

As he grabbed a muffin, he wobbled his finger and the butter slid within his reach. He spread a thick layer on top of the sweetbread. "Try as you may," Cole glanced at her, "and I don't want to know *how* you're trying—the Mother Earth Beads won't help you, Elaina."

His words struck her heart like a blunt knife. Their choice not to tell the family— the Sentinels—wrung her nerves every time they were mentioned. *Please, Vince, please find them this time.*

Cole looked her way.

You are so stupid, Elaina. Watch yourself. Elaina fidgeted and looked at the liquid in her cup. *Could he have heard that?* She peeked at him through her lashes.

He took a bite of his breakfast and then lifted his chin. His jaw worked the food as he leaned back, stretching his long legs in front of him. "It would be very bad to lose a magical item."

"Cole," James' firm voice struck Elaina's nerves, and her gaze snapped to him. "Elaina would tell us the moment they turned up missing. A simple scry would lead us to their location and we can summon them." He waved his hand and cake tins flew from the cabinet beside the oven to settle before the young twins. "Don't cause unneeded worry."

Heat rushed her face, and she pinched her lips together to control the quiver in her chin.

The receiving hall door slammed, and Cole leaned his forehead to Anna's. "I'll be back soon, my love."

Her fingers combed his black hair past his shoulders. "Don't be long."

"Never." He stood and motioned to James.

James tugged the towel from his broad shoulder and released the apron from his waist.

Elaina's heart sped and pounded against her rib cage. *He knows!* She swallowed the thickness in her throat. *Sweet, Venus. Please let Vince have found their father's cerulean beads.*

Though prayer to the foreign goddess held her hopes, she knew the slam of the door could only mean irritation at another failed try.

Chapter Three

"In the study. Now."

Cole's thoughts hit Vincent as he hung his cloak on the gold coatrack prong. His oldest brother's piqued stride hammered against the hardwood floor and echoed off the cherubim lined walls. His scowl bore into Vincent as he rounded the wide staircase, heading down the left hall.

James followed. His blink in Vincent's direction foretold this wasn't going to be a pleasant brotherly meet.

What's the old brood mad about this time? Vincent looked at the cascading chandelier with a heavy sigh. The teardrop gems seemed to reply with the possible answer in each twinkle. Unease flashed across his senses.

He clenched his jaw and followed, casting his gaze to the seraphim that stood sentinel beside the banister. Its cold features stared ahead as if ignoring his presence. Vincent grumbled under his breath. "A little support here would be nice."

Laurel trees framed the door to their

father's personal study, branches intertwined above the entrance. Plush carpet hushed their steps as they entered, and soft illumination poured from the bobbles along the top tier of the wall-sized bookshelf. Track lamps spotted the tapestries on the east wall, highlighting the intricate depictions of their home realm. The mantel shelves displayed the many magical items brought with them when they came to serve in Cornerstone Deep. Vincent glanced at the spot where the beads once lay. A pang of guilt knotted his stomach.

James waved his hand and the circular chandelier lit, bathing them with light.

As soon as Vincent closed the door, Cole's command rang in his ears.

"*Eko silyst.*"

The atmosphere thickened as the silencing spell entombed the room. Cole turned to him, and his ebony eyes flashed. His irritated tone flattened with each word as the tunnel effect allowed only those within the room to hear it. "How long have you known?"

James settled into the master chair behind the cherry-wood desk and leaned back. Vincent paused as the sight set another knot in his stomach. Would he ever get used to seeing James in the Head of

Sentinel's position? The reminder of Cole's demotion by the Gods set a grave tone in the air. A frown took the dimples from James' cheeks as he laced his fingers across his defined torso in the familiar counseling pose.

Vincent rested his hands at his waist and set his jaw. "Known what?"

Cole's eyes narrowed with his glare. Folding his arms, he shuffled his stance. The tempered air didn't hide the anger in his voice. "That your woman lost the Mother Earth beads that should have never been removed from this room."

The accusation grated Vincent's nerves alongside his earlier failed search. "Her name is Elaina!" He raked his fingers over his scalp and couldn't hold back his defensive argument. "From the time I announced our engagement, you've demeaned her importance to me. I love her more than any—"

"Of the twelve before her?" Cole's brow cocked, pressing the punch further.

Vincent's knuckles glowed hot as his fists bunched tight. "She's my soul mate!"

James glanced at them. "Cole has never demeaned those you've chosen to wed, Vince."

"Only the frequency," Cole murmured with a side sneer.

"I'm not spending my life in loneliness when we live thousands of years after they pass." The habitual response came before he could catch it, and Vincent lowered his gaze as he realized his error.

"Well, given light that we now know reincarnation exists on Cornerstone Deep, none of us will." James' softened tone seemed to hush Cole's harsh manner. "Now, I'd like to know the answer to Cole's question. When I suggested you allow Elaina to hold onto the beads for comfort, I fully expected to be notified if they came missing."

Vincent straightened his spine and blinked to the side. He knew it would come to this. With each empty scry result, he knew. His gaze wandered the pile in the thick carpet as he gnawed on his inner cheek. "She discovered they were missing the night we fought Dressen."

Cole growled, and his anger exploded in a telepathic burst along with his voice. "What? Three weeks? Three weeks have passed, and this is the *first* time you mention it?"

"If you'll remember, your attentions were on more pressing matters, like Dressen's death, upcoming memorial, and the gift you insist on forging for his sister. And Mianna... You wanted to do everything right to help her settle so you could plan the wedding you insisted on having last week..."

Frustration gnawed at Vincent's gut. "And all James thinks about is his new family. Every day Elaina is around those girls, she wants a child more. It's become an obsession!"

He tossed his hand through the air and unrestrained sparks flew from his fingertips. "I've spent the last three weeks searching this realm for those beads with her checking in with me every chance she gets. When I have to tell her they can't be found, she breaks into tears."

Cole paced until he stood before the hearth. "They won't do a thing to help her have a child."

"Of course, they won't! And I don't know how many times I've tried to reason with her. But she won't hear it."

James leaned forward, resting his elbows on the desk, and Vincent wasn't sure if he saw anger or concern etched on his brow. "You've scryed for them?"

By his tone, Vincent was sure it was concern. "Yes. Nothing." He shook his head. "I was confused, too."

"When was the last time she remembers having them?"

"At Shilo Park, when Mianna went into

the High Priest's buggy with Dressen. She unwound them from her wrist to call me for help on her watch. She said she was sure she put them in her pocket."

Cole's gaze shot over his shoulder. "She did this when Dressen was there? Did he see her do it?"

Vincent considered. A slow shrug held his shoulders arched. "Possibly."

Cole rolled his head to the side and walked in a small circle. "He was using the memory pearl I gave him to view his past lives at the time. Father's life cycle was at the forefront of his mind. If he saw them, he recognized them. He had to have taken them."

A sneer tugged at Vincent's cheek. "Without her noticing?"

Cole cocked his head and lifted his hand toward the picture window on the far side of the room. The golden rope gracefully untied, allowing the drapes to flow closed. It snaked through the air into Cole's palm. Tassels bunched between his fingers as he snapped them into a fist.

Blood drained from Vincent's face as he realized how easily the beads could have slipped from her pocket and into Dressen's hand under a command.

James stood, his bulky arms down at his sides. "Magical items in the possession of a wizard," he took a deep breath, "follow that soul when it dies."

A furrow bit deep into Vincent's brow as he hoped beyond fact it wasn't true. "So..."

Cole confirmed his fear. "So, the beads *and* the memory pearl are somewhere on Midway Summit." His upper lip curled. "Where the one man with the ability to recall them was reborn!"

Vincent snapped in his love's defense. "She had nothing to do with that pearl!"

James' dark eyes widened, and he swallowed so hard Vincent could hear it squelch. "I was under the impression you had retrieved the ring," he seemed to struggle to get the last word out, "Cole."

Cole thrust the decorative rope to the floor and then raked his fingers over his head. "I intended to get it from him. I tried, and I almost had it when..." He looked at the tassel slumped in a heap at his feet. His shoulders drooped, and his voice lowered. "When I realized the severity of my actions. I failed."

James shook his head. "Nobody could have known Dressen's life would be taken."

Cole gave him a sidelong glance and voiced Vincent's own thoughts. "And that's supposed to make me feel better?"

With a sigh, James reclaimed his seat and looked at his hands. "You need to know something."

The room fell silent and the pause seemed to stretch the air thin. Forebodings sent chills across Vincent's skin as he watched James lace and then tighten his fingers. Vincent's nostrils flared with the twitch of stomach muscles.

"When I led Dressen's soul to his next life, I was very careful to follow Taravaughn's instruction." James swallowed again and then licked his lips. Puffing his cheeks outward until they deflated, he exhaled a mouthful of air. The corners of his mouth drew down.

For the first time in his life, Vincent saw a concern in his brother's countenance so deep that it melted his face to putty.

"There were ten Selvite birthing chambers in use. All would have given him the opportunity to learn humility and loyalty, simply by being born to those in service. But..." His gaze lifted, and he breathed deep, causing his broad chest to expand and his large pectorals to look twice their size. "I found one that lost her child during birth. The woman's cry wasn't at the loss of her child. It was at the inability to serve her master's needs...a continued line of service." He shook his head. "She was too small and probably failed at giving birth in the past."

Cole's brow dipped. "James, you didn't show yourself to help this woman, did you?"

"His mother will have a clear mind to teach him what he needs to learn, and he'll gain it through pure service." He looked back at his hands as his voice trail off. "His father named him Allant."

Vincent quirked his cheek. "Doesn't that mean High One?"

James nodded, and Cole's breath rushed from his lips.

"So, you *did* show yourself."

"I weighed the outcomes. It was the truest path I could find for him." James' tone lowered to just above a whisper. "I had no idea he'd name him after the High Ones. Or that the items transferred with him."

Cole's features hardened to the point Vincent thought the tables might turn, and he'd be the one to temper his brother instead of the other way around. Cole took a deep breath and squared his shoulders. "You realize how naming the child after a High One could change their view of their lot in life. They're slaves!"

James closed his eyes. "How could I have known?"

Vincent folded his arms, irritation replacing the dread. "Okay. What's going on?"

He looked at each in turn. How much did they know about all of this, anyway? Yet another subject his father chose to share with his older brothers while he learned at his mother's side? He cursed his soul's short existence. He may be living his first lifespan, but that didn't mean he was incompetent.

A rap came at the door, and Cole stiffened with a huff. "*Coneko silyst.*" The room returned to its noisy freedom as he marched to the entrance and flung it wide. "What is it?"

Linda set her hand on her voluptuous hip. "No need to be testy. You have a guest." She thumbed toward the receiving hall and glanced at James with a small smirk. "I never thought I'd say this, but this guy rivals you, honey."

James' brows bit into a deep furrow.

She nodded. "Yeah, muscles and all."

He jumped to a stand, and Cole's jaw dropped, replacing his scowl. "James, you wait here."

Vincent matched Cole's long strides as they passed the laurel-twined entrance and continued down the hall to the foyer. Broken sentences punched into Vincent's mind, and he realized the extent of Cole's unease. His brother wasn't harnessing the voice of his thoughts. The words came in broken fragments; *Uncle...centuries...*hide *her?*

As they rounded the marble staircase seraphim, Cole stopped with a jolt, and Vincent sidestepped to keep from bumping into him. He gazed past his brother and had to look twice at what he saw.

The large man knelt before Mechenzie and gently braced her elbows with his thick hands. Her gray eyes darkened to onyx, and awe crossed his flushed features.

A breath passed the visitor's lips with one word. "Lilith."

Chapter Four

Vincent cocked his head in disbelief. "Uncle Rhune?"

A large hand grasped his shoulder, shoving him aside, and James' voice boomed in his ears. "Unhand her!"

Vincent flinched at the force.

His brother's broad frame marched a step before him, and his muscles bulged to the point of stretching the fabric of his shirt. James took a wide stance and then backhanded the air, fingers clawed.

Rhune flew from the little girl in a great arch. His cape flattened to his back, and he stepped mid-air as his head collided with the cascading chandelier. Crystals clanked, the two-story lamp swayed, and several gems broke away, clattering onto the hardwood floor. Rhune dispersed his elements before he could land on the banister and hovered, partially visible. Righting himself, he stood three feet above the steps. His cloak flowed through his essence, settling around him.

He looked at James, a hint of sorrow showing in his dark eyes. As he solidified, he lowered to the middle of the staircase.

Linda rushed to Mechenzie's side, but James' long strides reached her first. He scooped the little girl into his arms and pulled her into a protective hold. "How dare you present yourself to her. She's a child!"

His warning nearly drowned out her mother's soft, "Are you okay?"

Rhune held out his hands. "I meant no harm, Jamesuranton. I only wanted to..." He dropped them to his sides. "You boys keep terrible records. Your Vignette entries are so sporadic that I didn't learn of Lilith's death until Vincentor gave his account of what happened with your Lord Dressen and who he really was."

A scowl tightened James' lips. "So, you rush here to claim a six-year-old."

Rhune shook his head. "I came to see if you'd found her. None of you made mention in your reports. I searched Meridian, expecting to find she'd returned, but there was no sign of her there." He nodded to the little girl in James' arms. "She answered the door with her mother."

Linda flushed and looked at James as she reached for Mechenzie. "Why don't I take her to check the cake?"

James hesitated, but then released her to her mother's arms.

Vincent looked from James to Cole and then back. Was he the only one itching to grab his uncle into a rough-kin hug? They hadn't seen him in nearly six hundred years, and when he comes to Cornerstone Deep, all he gets is a power punch that lands him on the marble-capped stairs? Could there possibly be something else he was left out of in the past?

He looked at the man. His brilliant maroon cape flared from the tall collar, pleated into a tailored fit across his broad shoulders. The light fabric fell to cover his wide torso and brushed his thighs. His close-fitted trousers couldn't hide the definition in his legs and hugged his ankles above what looked like seal skin shoes. He definitely didn't use them for walking.

The peculiar thought sent a twinge of humor through Vincent's heart, and he scoffed to himself. Of course, he hadn't. What Meridian walked any distance?

Ignoring his brothers' cold welcome, he bypassed Cole and trotted up the steps to Rhune. A bright smile bloomed on his uncle's face the closer he got. Grasping his shoulders, Vincent growled and wrapped his arms around the hulking man. "Uncle Rhune. It's so good to see you!"

With a chuckle, their closest relative returned the heart-felt greeting and patted him on the back with a heavy hand. "Vincent, my boy. As it is you." His gaze returned to James and his smile mellowed. "As it is all of you."

~ * ~

Elaina pulled the cakes from the oven as Linda's quick steps patted into the kitchen. A quirked expression covered her sister's face, and she seemed reluctant to let Mechenzie go.

"Who was at the door?"

Linda bit her lips together. "I take it the guys' uncle, Rhune."

Anna's bright eyes flashed as she tore her gaze from her rings. "He's here from Meridian?"

"You know him?"

"Only because Sylis mentioned him, and I asked Cole about it. They don't talk about him much." She stood and placed her drink in the tri-tub sink. "I gathered something happened a long time ago. He put a lot on the line by helping Sylis and Lilith out with a situation on Midway Summit. It kind of eased tensions but..."

Elaina's attention snapped to the topic, and the tins slipped from her grasp.

Mechenzie's little hand shot out as if to catch them in her open palm. They halted and hovered in the air.

"Oh," Elaina gasped, and grabbed them, setting them on the stove. "Mechenzie, thank you. You're such a lifesaver."

Her chipmunk cheeks pooched with her smile. "You're welcome, Auntie Elaina. I like to do that."

"Aww." Her head tilted as dreams of her future family came back. "Someday, when Uncle Vincent and I have children, you'll have cousins to show how it's done. And then you can all make things go through the air."

As Mechenzie giggled, Mandy dashed to her and grabbed her hand. "Come on, Kenzie. You can do it now with *me*. You can show *me* how to do it."

Mechenzie rolled her eyes. "You can't do magic."

Her twin's lip pouted. "I can watch you."

Linda set Mechenzie down and shooed them toward the back door. "Go on, have fun."

As the two darted out the back door, Elaina returned her attention to Anna. "Did the guys tell you about Midway? What's it like? What did Sylis do there?"

Anna quirked her cheek and shook her head. "I don't really know what he did, but it's all related to the people that ended up there when they breached the portal on Earth."

Linda folded her arms and appeared as interested in the subject as Elaina. "You mean Earth, as in Cornerstone Summit? He was involved with all that?"

"I don't think he had anything to do with the breach, but he and Lilith both loved the cornerstone realms. Especially Earth. Sylis did talk about that. I got the impression he'd much rather have been assigned there instead of here on Terra."

An impatient nod overtook Elaina, and she swirled her hand to get Anna to continue.

"They didn't know how to travel the realms," Anna added as she gathered the leftover snacks. "I take it they were lost for quite some time. But, the Council was furious that they even got that far. The Sentinels stationed on Earth sealed the portal, so even if they knew how, they couldn't have gone back. By the time they reached Moraine—that's the familiar name for Midway Summit, by the way—a lot of them were near death."

Linda voiced Elaina's own shock. "Near death?"

Anna tilted her head and looked to the side. "As soon as Sylis heard about it all, he told Lilith and called on Rhune. They needed to use the Triad of Purpose to save them."

"Wow."

"Well..." Anna wiped her hands on a towel. "He'll need a place to sleep. And I doubt he dressed for the colder climate."

"Unless there's some kind of spell in those threads." A snort burst from Linda's lips as she grinned. "You should see his clothes. It's like their painted on. And that cape is purely ornamental."

Elaina rushed to their side, unable to contain the excitement. "That's right. Meridian is way hotter than it is here."

Cole shuffled into the room, and Anna's countenance brightened, despite his scowl. As she hooked her arms around his waist, he leaned his head to the side and gazed at her bright eyes. His irritation seemed to ebb, the tension in his brow eased as she spoke.

"Oh, Cole. Your uncle's visiting all the way from Meridian? How grand! Our first houseguest. I'll show him to the newly decorated guest bedroom on the second floor. I can't wait to show it off."

"My love." He brushed the dark waves from her face with a gentle stroke. "I think we should have him stay in one of the third-floor rooms."

Anna's smile faded. "Oh, no, that won't do. I haven't had time to work on them yet."

Linda's blonde brows lifted, and she cocked her head. "Well, you may want to put him on the far end, Anna. It's obvious James doesn't like him at all. And I don't think Cole's keen on his visit either. Vince seemed the only one willing to welcome him."

Cole glanced at her, and Anna tipped on her toes, kissing him on the nose.

"Okay. The far end it is." Her shoes clip-clopped against the tile floor as she headed for the foyer. "And I'll find him a set of clothes to wear to Lord Dressen's memorial. Won't the noblemen be surprised?" She ended her exit with a stumble and a mild curse about big feet before she disappeared.

A frown crossed Cole's face as he hesitated and looked around. The aimless gesture proved he didn't like the idea, and Elaina wondered if he'd ever deny Anna anything that made her happy. So far, Vincent's assessment of the two reuniting had proven spot on. With a shuffle, he followed his love.

Elaina dipped her brows into a deep V, and she grabbed Linda's arm. "Only Vince welcomed him?"

Linda shook her head with a chuckle. "Rhune was talking to Kenzie when James came into the foyer. He completely threw him across the room."

"James?"

"You should have seen it. It was a complete wizard moment. A wave of his hand and the man flew through the air. Rhune shifted into a ghost and his cape settled through his...body until it was straight. Then he floated right onto the stairs with grace. Could have sworn I was watching a special-effects movie."

Linda upped her brow. "Hope Rhune didn't decide to take a tour of Shilo before he got here." She chuckled again. "He'd draw more attention in his getup than when Gryffin was missing from his perch."

"Why in the world would James do that?"

Linda shrugged. "I was more concerned about how tight he was holding Kenzie. His arms were bulging, and she was flat against his chest."

Elaina's thoughts reeled to another direction. "Do you think that's why he came? Their gods wanted her to come back to Meridian."

Linda flushed. "Taravaughn promised she could stay." She shook her head with a defiant jerk, and her arms folded tight around her bosom. "They're not getting her. Nothing's going to take her away from me."

Elaina looked out the wide window of the breakfast nook. Light stretched across the terrace from the kitchen and highlighted the twins as they darted around the marble statues. Long shadows danced in their wake and blended with the darkness beyond the landing.

Should she remind Linda of the last time she had made such a statement? "Linda, I don't want them to take Kenzie either, but you know..."

"No!"

Elaina closed her eyes, hoping with all her heart that it wasn't true, but considering the circumstances, what else could it be?

Chapter Five

The parlor door swung open to darkness as Rhune neared the threshold. He hesitated, second-guessing his decision to enter. Scanning the quiet receiving hall, he lifted his gaze to the ceiling three stories above. The chandelier twinkled as it hung from the high arc and cascaded to be level with the second landing. It was there he'd last embraced his brother. It was there all resentment had been buried.

He leaned his head to look past the open door. A narrow band of light illuminated the plush carpet and gleamed across the cherry-wood bar. The counter served as a stout foundation for the wall-sized liqueur selection above it. The bottles seemed to assess him in a variety of muted hues, standing proudly on the ornate gold-trimmed shelves.

He glanced at the door, and it opened wider with his thought command. Deep shadows stretched from the nearby leather chairs and rose to hide the lower half of the large hearth on the far wall. The dark wood braced an amber marble mantle, swirls pressed into the material like thick claws artfully played there. The portrait of Sylis Shilo hung over it and filled the space, leaving only room for the cherubs to peak over the edges from their places along the ceiling. Flexing his fingers, he rubbed his hands together to dispel the chill and then stepped inside.

With a glance at the cast iron grate in the fireplace, the neatly piled logs burst into flames. Heat poured through the room with the tang of burnt oak, and he relaxed a measure as he sank into the sofa. The soft cushions welcomed him with a low *creak*.

He looked around the room as the added illumination highlighted the surfaces and danced along the walls. The exclamatory mirror on the east side reflected the flames and cast the illusion of a magical photo of the room. His gaze traced his brother's portrait within the semblance.

He blinked and dipped his hand into his shirt pocket. Pinching his thumb and forefinger together, he caused the tip of his Lotus Lines to appear. Four long-stemmed straws materialized as he pulled them out, and he leaned his head, considering the strength he'd require. Joy? Serenity? Sleep? Certainly not exotic. A light flavor would do for this evening, though upon arrival, he had expected a stronger taste would have been needed. He chose a serene P-Lotus and stashed the rest from where they came.

As he nipped the tip, a soft mist pooled around his lips, seeped into his nerve endings, and coated the pleasure senses in his brain. His cares ebbed with the whirl of jolly dancing in his mind.

He leaned back, crossing an ankle over his knee, and took another nip. A heavy sigh passed his lips and then he looked back to his brother's depiction. The square features stared at him with a baronial air.

"Four hundred years." Rhune's voice rumbled in his throat alongside the slight sway of his mind. "I should have known something wasn't right when the boys took over the Vignette's Chronicle entries." He rolled his jaw and then set it. "I didn't know, Sylisan. I'm truly sorry." He lowered his gaze to the Lotus. "And as for Lilith's death... I half expected *you* to avoid mentioning it. But..."

"He asked us not to."

Colhart's low voice washed over him, and he blinked toward the doorway. The foyer's brightness framed his nephew's silhouette as he lifted from his lean on the frame. He went to the bar and poured himself a drink.

"Kid didn't know that, though. Father never included him in the Sentinel duties...or the reason to exclude the information."

Rhune nodded and looked back down at his P-Lotus. "So, I could have gone some millennia without knowing."

Colhart took a drink and sank into a leather chair, stretching his long legs in front of him. "I trust your room is satisfactory. Mianna tells me you've settled into one she recently decorated."

Change of subject. A small puff of air passed Rhune's nostrils, and he drew a breath, accepting a congenial conversation instead. "Oh, yes. Aside from the chill, it's comfortable enough."

Colhart grinned. "I'll get you one of James' cloaks and sleep ware."

Rhune nodded. "I forgot how much colder it is in the cornerstone realms. But, there's no need, Colhart. The Terran woman provided a set."

"Her name is Mianna."

Cocking his head, he considered. "Mianna is the brunette you chose to spend time with, isn't that right?"

The grin on Colhart's lips faded, and he looked at him. "Mianna is my soul mate, Uncle Rhune. Not a simple bed partner."

Rhune blinked as if the words shot air at his eyes. *Surely not.*

He studied his nephew's demeanor for a hint of humor, but Colhart offered no light-hearted expression. Onyx eyes stared back, steady.

Rhune pursed his lips and nipped at the tip of his Lotus. "You've claimed a woman of Cornerstone Deep as an eternal companion?"

"All souls are eternal and progress."

"Well, yes, of course." He furrowed his brow. "But..." *He can't be serious.*

Colhart lifted his chin.

"Their lives are the measure of a day compared to ours. Their advancement is that of a child." A chuckle bubbled in his chest, and he let it curve his lips as much to lighten the weight of Colhart's stare as to recall the moment. "Such as the one who showed me to my room. The redhead. Very inquisitive. I don't think I've ever met a woman with more questions in over three thousand years."

"That would be Elaina." Colhart's head eased into a lean. "And Vincent's soul mate."

Unable to control the reaction, air rushed from Rhune's lungs. *Surely, not!* He cleared his throat. *They've served this post far too long if they've come to this.*

A scowl flashed across Colhart's face.

Rhune flexed his leg muscles as he stretched them out in front of him with a relaxing growl. "Ah, well. Once you return to Meridian, things will most likely settle into place. I'm sure equal soul mates will surface."

The tone in Colhart's voice stiffened and lowered to a challenge. "Soul mates are eternal. You know this."

He did know it. But nothing in the Arched Spectrum of Realms would convince him that his nephews hadn't made a terrible mistake by opening their souls to foreign women. "So, you're telling me that even if a soul of the Midway realms had called to you, you would have answered and locked your progression to the equivalent of a newborn." He shook his head with a cocked smile. "They're priceless—don't get me wrong, but as simple as they come."

Colhart's hand tightened around his glass. "Eternal progression isn't determined by physical abilities. And technology has nothing to do with what a soul must learn."

Rhune slowly nodded. *Okay. This woman's got him tied in deep.* He lifted a brow and hoped the plea didn't show in his tone. "And Jamesuranton?"

"He's courting Linda. He plans to wed her when the time is right."

"So, they'll be together until she passes." *Please tell me this is true.*

"Yes."

Thank the Gods!

Colhart shot to a stand, setting his drink on the table beside him with a clunk. "I should inform you that my abilities have grown since we last met. I'm able to perceive thoughts." The plush carpet couldn't hide the irritation in his long strides as he headed to the door. "I'll bid you a good night."

Rhune pursed his lips and upped his brows. *Nice. At least the ancient lifestyle hasn't hampered his advancement.*

The door slammed.

Glancing up to the portrait above the hearth, he shook his head. "They're your sons."

~ * ~

"Vince, he told me all about her. She's a Goddess to Midway Summit. And she adores being prayed to. Especially about children. She loves to grant that prayer." Elaina's enthusiasm added to his joy of his uncle's visit.

"He's my favorite relative, and he loves

to talk about the gods." The warm comforter enveloped him as he crawled into bed beside her. "Used to take me on his knee and tell stories. We'd sit there for hours." He smiled and cuddled close, pulling her into an embrace. "Father never took the time. He always had some business to attend to with Cole and James. But, Uncle Rhune more than made up for it. He had me and Mother laughing all the time."

"Did you know that all he had to do was enter the portal and think of Cornerstone Deep and start walking? Brought him right here."

He chuckled and nuzzled her ear. "I've traveled the portal, Elaina. I know how it all works."

She twirled a curl around her finger, and her gaze seemed to follow images in her mind. "I figured there was some big magical spell or something you had to do to make it work. If it's that easy, how is it that others don't use it?"

Vincent paused and looked at her face more fully. She really wanted to talk right now? From the time he left to search for the beads, she'd end their calls with promises of intimate acts he never thought she was capable of performing. Those acts dominated his mind and drove him harder to find the charms, so he could return as soon as possible. He hitched his leg around hers.

"Well, for one thing, few know of the portal. And of those few, none know of the realms, other than Meridian. Nobody enters Meridian unless they hold a Meridian soul. That is, unless led there by one who does. Besides, only we know the portal's location."

Her face scrunched into excitement. "This is all so amazing!" She turned to face him. "Vince, I can't believe all of this exists. It's really real. Venus is real. And she loves to grant prayers to those who desire children."

Unease heated Vincent's stomach. "Elaina, you have your own gods. Your veneration should go to them." He traced her cheek with his forefinger as he looked deep into her soul. "Gryffin, Taravaughn, and Arylin are very worthy of your prayers. They created you. You're their child. They know what's best for you."

Elaina's sweet smile sent sparks to her loving eyes. "But I'm married to a Meridian man. A glorious, wonderful, chosen soul who travels the realms. That has to mean that more gods are involved in our lives." She placed her hand on his jaw and kissed him with a feather touch. Then, for the first time since they'd said their vows, she rolled over, pulling his arm around her.

Confusion morphed his mind. Where was the heated embrace? The desperate clinging? The proclamations of love? He kissed her strawberry hair, pulling her to him. With a deep breath, he ground his hips against her and savored the dip of her firm buttocks against his groin. Heat pulsed in his core.

"Elaina," he said with a breath.

"Hmm?"

"I've been gone, searching for Father's beads." He led his lips to her neck and slid his hand along her abdomen, allowing the softness and warmth of her skin to heighten his desire.

"Oh, Vince. I really am so tired. And it's going to be a big day tomorrow with Rhune here." She peeked at him from the corner of her eye. "Let's get some sleep. Okay?"

Sleep? Is she serious?

As she settled into her pillow, she cupped his hand with hers, halting the tender caresses.

Shock rushed him. *Dear, Gods. She is!*

~ * ~

James glanced down the hall to ensure an empty corridor and then turned to watch

Linda tuck the Clifford the Clown comforter around the twins. The image of the purple fringed-topped friend slept within the threads of muted tones, while the worn, true-to-life doll slumped between the twins lying against matching pillowcases. Entirely too much clown for James' liking, but they had been thrilled when he gave the birthday gift to them two days early.

A grin played on his lips as their mother placed kisses on their foreheads. The scene warmed his heart...clowns and all.

He stepped to Linda's side, watching the sweet moment. As she rose from Momma huggles, he bent and pressed a kiss to each blonde head. His heart swelled as four little arms reached up and held his neck in a brief hug.

"Nighty-night, Poppa James," chimed Mechenzie. Mandy followed with the same sentiment.

"Nighty-night, girls." He smiled and wondered when his voice had taken on such a silly sounding melody when he spoke to them.

James and Linda stepped across the ingress, and he closed the door with a soft click. As she took his hand and headed toward their room at the end of the hall, he paused. "Perhaps we should stay in the room across from them tonight."

Linda frowned, and her blue gaze met his. "What's wrong? You don't think he'd really do anything to hurt Kenzie, do you?"

He straightened, squaring his shoulders. "Hurt her? No, not hurt."

A heavy crease bit between her blonde brows. "James, it's obvious you don't trust him. If he wouldn't hurt her... Why is he here, anyway? Was he sent to take her back to Meridian? Because if he is..."

James looked into her eyes and saw the protective flare he loved.

"I don't care if he is from the highest, magical, most ancient, advance dimension there is. He's not taking her. I won't let him."

Her grip tightened on his hand as she spoke, and her nails dug into the top of his palm. He kissed her fingertips to call her attention to the action.

Her gaze didn't vary as she loosened her hold. A tone of reason replaced the anger in her voice. "James, he'll be going against Taravaughn. He can't go against a God. Surely, your gods will stand by the decisions of ours. I mean they're all Gods—younger dimension or not." A deep frown pressed her full lips together as she stuffed her hand inside her pocket. "And so help me... If Taravaughn doesn't stop him, I swear, I will. Whatever it takes."

Tears moistened her eyes, and she shook her head as she removed a slender cigarette and lighter. She lit the tip and drew a quick puff. Discarded smoke lifted to exit through the charm induced conduit James had placed on the pack.

"I don't care what they'll do to me. They can't take my baby from me."

He set his hand on her shoulder and shook his head. "The gods uphold decisions made. Taravaughn said he will allow her to stay as long as our gods wish it. So, he won't be able to take her through the portal without our gods' command. And we haven't been notified of such an arrangement." His lips curled with the disgust that boiled in his gut, knowing there were ways around that law. "I'll make sure he never looks at her again."

Linda's complexion drained. "James?"

He scanned the portraits that lined the walls. The entire Shilo family was portrayed with the exception of Rhune Avier Hru Eshnal Shilomacj. As far as he knew, his uncle's depiction still nestled in the dark corner of the cellar, tightly bound in heavy paper and cords.

Smoke billowed and then veered to flow out the slight hole above the cigarette as her whisper carried an insecure pitch. "What has he done?"

James heaved a lengthy breath. Could he even say it after all the years of silencing the matter? Of denying the fact?

He pressed his lips into a line and slowly shook his head. Softening his expression, he brushed a few stray locks from her face. "Not now, Leenja. One day, perhaps. But, not now."

He lightly kissed her worried brow and then took her hand, leading her to the room across the way.

One night would be all he would allow the man in this realm; one night to rest from his travels. Elaina and Mianna may dote on him during breakfast, but then, he would see Rhune Shilomacj to the portal himself.

Chapter Six

Clinks and scuffs carried through the hall as Vincent neared the kitchen. The scent of sweetened cinnamon filled the air, alongside fresh coffee, and he filled his lungs with the homey aroma. Stepping into the room, he paused. If he hadn't known better, he'd swear he'd stepped back in time to his childhood.

Light blue sunbeams poured through the indigo-charmed nook window, creating rainbow starbursts on the polished cookware above the kitchen island. Whisks whipped ingredients alongside cutlery that sliced fruit, each bite-sized piece taking its place in a nearby bowl. The oven door opened, and a sheet of rolls emerged. The sweetbreads lifted and settled on a platter as the tin returned to the cabinet, baked remains dissolving to leave it sparkling clean as if washed. The whisk tapped the edge of the mixing bowl with three sharp clinks and then paused in the air as the container tipped, drizzling icing onto the breads.

The coffee pot flew through the room from the percolator, heading toward the hall, and Vincent grabbed the handle as it passed. The sweetbread followed suit, and he allowed it to lead the way out the door.

Laughter flowed from the dining hall, and he smiled to himself.

Of course, Uncle Rhune.

As Vincent stepped into the room, the drapes parted from the large windows in a grandiose display, tassels tying the fabric up to mimic a grand stage. An opalescent sheen morphed the glass blue, causing the sun's rays to darken and spill indigo light from the far wall. The cherry-wood dining set glowed deep red while mute tones reflected on the gold tray at the center. Bobbles, held suspended by the same golden material, dimmed and the larger three hanging over the center of the room hazed with a meandering mist.

A wide smile spread across Rhune's face, and then he lifted his hands toward the door, eyes sparkling. "Vincent, my boy! Come in. Your little Terran butterfly has been entertaining me with her questions."

Mianna laughed and picked up a treat as the platter lighted on the table before them. "More like Rhune has been entertaining us. I don't remember you guys mentioning how charming he is."

"Uncle Rhune?" Vincent placed the coffee on the table and folded his arms with a scoff. "He could talk a mouse out of its cheese."

A one syllable laugh carried through the air as Rhune tossed his head back. His shoulders bounced as lively chuckles followed with a playful edge. The man, as big if not bigger, than James, put on a larger than life show in his colorful cape, wavy hair, and broad mouth of shiny teeth. Mianna and Elaina joined in with high-pitched giggles, and the joyful moment burst through the room.

Elaina's freckles seemed darker against her pale skin as she smiled so hard her cheeks pressed arches into her eyes. "How long are you planning to stay with us, Uncle Rhune?"

"Oh, I don't know," he said, mellowing. "It's dangerous to wear out a welcome, especially at one of the Shilo Manors. Sentinels have duties to concentrate on now, isn't that right?"

Elaina leaned farther over the table. "One of the Shilo Manors? You mean there are more?"

"Oh, sure there are. On each dimension in the spectrum. The Sentinels need a place to call home, don't they?"

"I guess so." Humor laced her words. "Are they all the same? Just like this one? Do they have the same protective charms? The magical items? The white trees surrounding them that bloom all year round? What about the—?"

Rhune's laughter rang, cutting off Elaina's intensive questioning. "Vincent, my boy, you do have an inquisitive girl here."

A smile crept up Vincent's right cheek. That he did, and though he had to admit it was bothersome at times, he couldn't help being proud of the fact. Questions led to understanding and understanding led to growth. He propped his leg on the table in a leaning sit as he observed Rhune filling her in on the matter.

"Let me see if I can put a dent into sedating your curiosity, Terran butterfly. The manors are the same. The original stands on Chenal hillside, facing Quelmacj sea. When Sylisan's family was called to fill the first Sentinel triad position, the family home was christened and endowed." He lifted his finger and tilted his head toward her. "At that moment, the gods parted the veils to the realms, and each accepted a shadow of that hallowed home, along with certain items that aid in the Sentinel's duties. The Utopian, Vignette, tapestries..."

He shifted in his seat and rested back into his chair. "While all the manors are protected within a band of enchantment to cause forgetfulness to any unauthorized person who wanders near, dear Lilith cast her own protective charms on this house. She couldn't bear the thought of her treasured items being affected by the elements of the foreign worlds—whether shadows of them or not."

"Forgetfulness?" Elaina's brows rose, causing her forehead to wrinkle. "Linda said when she came up here her thoughts were all over the place. She had to keep reminding herself the guys would help her get Mandy and Mechenzie back. So, that was why?"

Vincent nodded. "If someone is really determined, they can get past the cloud of confusion. If they're just curious, it generally breaks their interest."

Rhune's gaze lowered. "And the trees bloom year-round in case the blossoms are needed to carry a Meridian soul to his next life."

Elaina voiced her awe with a breath. "Wow."

Mianna placed her hand on Rhune's thick arm. "Well, don't you even think about rushing off. You're family. You stay as long as you like."

His brows rose as he placed his hands on the table, palm side down. "The rest of the family may have a say in that."

"But you haven't seen Shilo. You must let us show you the city. It's so amazing! So many wonders."

Tilting his head, he peered at Mianna. "I remember Cole's description of you so many years ago. Do you yet see all of life as a game, my little Terran angel?"

"Her name is Mianna." Cole's heavy tone carried from behind Vincent. "You may address her as an equal here."

Rhune nodded and looked at his hands. "I meant no disrespect, Colhart."

Vincent wrinkled his nose and glanced over his shoulder to sneer at the old brood. "He wasn't insulting her. The Uncle Rhune I know always uses pet names. They're endearing." He looked at the man seated at the end of the table, bathed in blue light and framed by the parted curtains. "It's when he doesn't use them that you need to worry."

Rhune chuckled.

Cole grunted and shuffled to leave. "Rhune. Kid. We need to talk. James is waiting in the study."

Chapter Seven

Cole's feet scuffed along the hardwood floor as Vincent and Rhune fell into step behind him. Crisp thuds echoed off the foyer walls as they rounded the staircase sentinels, and Cole wondered when he'd adjusted his strides to match theirs.

As he opened the study door, James swiveled in the master chair, facing them, and then leaned back and steepled his fingers over his waist. Cole still wasn't sure he cared for the sight of his brother at the Head Sentinel position, though he had every right to be there. His gaze shifted to the three Triad globes sitting along the front of the desk, and then the Utopian at the center behind them. He ran his palm down his chest to ease the knot that formed.

Out of habit, if not to give himself something to do, he cocked the counselor chair to the side and settled into the cushions, stretching his legs out in front of him.

Vincent entered the room, side-stepped, assuming his customary lean on the wall, and then crossed his arms as if bracing his chest.

James lowered his gaze before Rhune appeared, and Cole watched from his periphery as the man crossed the threshold and then walked around the back of Cole's chair on his way to the other. Cole scoffed to himself at the obvious attempt to avoid stepping over his legs...or not wanting to chance Cole's refusal to move.

James waved at the door, and it closed with a soft click. A slow sigh breezed through his lips as he quietly issued the silencing spell. *"Eko silyst."*

The air thickened and filled the room with auditory sealant.

Rhune eased into his seat with a glance at James. His gaze shifted to Cole, and then back. Cole expected the obvious question, *Shouldn't Cole be seated at the Head of Sentinels' position?*

"Thank you for including me in your discussions, Cole," his uncle said in a low tone.

Cole's jaw flexed as he stared straight ahead, and Vincent lowered his chin.

James laced his fingers. "I included you because I was instructed to do so."

"I see." Rhune's body filled the counselor chair as he leaned into it. "I take it more has happened that I don't know about."

Foregoing explanations, James waved his finger at the Utopian, and the mirrors rose in turn to create the tulip shaped stage. He spoke clearly. "Colhart Nixtoro Krylu Shilomacj, you are present here today to receive instruction from the Counsel concerning the sentencing of offenses to the Covenant. Rhune Avier Hru Eshnal Shilomacj, you are present here today to receive information from the Counsel concerning assignment. Please assume the required stand in show of respect."

Cole rose, squared his shoulders, clasped his hands behind his back, and then lifted his chin.

Rhune blinked several times and glanced at each of his nephews in turn.

James leaned forward and rested his arms on the desk.

Cole moved his eyes just enough to catch Rhune in his side vision. Surely the man heard what James had said. Silencing spell or not, he'd spoken with absolute clarity.

The new Head of Sentinels looked at his hands as he folded them. "The Counsel will not appear until proper respect is given."

"But what would the Counsel want with me? I've lived a respectable life. Traveled the realms, unearthing the secrets of ancient civilizations. If it weren't for me, they'd never have discovered the origins of that band of Roendaugh on Midway Deep."

A scoff caught in Cole's throat. "And Cornerstone Summit would have never heard of waters that revitalized life."

James held up his hand, palm pointed toward their uncle. "Please assume the position."

With another glance around, Rhune slowly stood and then mimicked Cole's stance.

A glow grew from deep within the crystal globes and created a mystical aura. The gleam from the circular chandeliers that hugged the ceiling, the track lights spotting the tapestries along the east wall, and the bulbs that capped the book shelves slowly dimmed. In a flash, a beam shot from the center of each globe and hit the three mirrors of the Utopian. A sheen of transparent film fluttered along the shafts as the reflectors slowly angled outward and a hologram came to life, filling the space between the desk and ceiling.

Several familiar souls, adorned with silver shoulder capes and tall golden collars, appeared, sitting on the three-tiered officiator stand of the Triad Court counsel. Age had claimed their youthful countenances, and Cole reeled at the reality. Four hundred years spent on Cornerstone Deep behind the locked door to the realms was short compared to Meridian. The speed at which the portal carried a traveler seemed to throw logic out of the equation. While the average Meridian lived to be well over ten-thousand years old, to them he'd reached nearly six of that and aged little. In truth, he was surprised to see so many Counselors that he knew were still in high rank. Time changed people. He could attest to that.

The shine from the ornate bronze crowns that capped the high-backed chairs cast a mild halo above the heads of the members and reminded Cole how closely these people worked with the gods.

He pressed his heals into the plush carpet to anchor himself against what his future held. They couldn't take him from Mianna, he knew that. The gods of Cornerstone Deep had declared their judgment for him to serve her for the rest of his soul's existence. That couldn't be denounced. Ethereal law ruled observance to their stand. As long as he had her, he could handle it.

Cole clenched his jaw and lifted his chin a little higher. *You deserve whatever they've decided.*

Theonis stepped into the picture from the right and faced him, clasping his hands over his long silver robe. Spokesman for the Counsel, his deep voice carried through the room, despite the silencing spell.

"Colhart, it has been five-thousand years since last we spoke, and you stand before me as one millennia at most. I see Cornerstone Deep time has been very kind to you."

Cole offered a small smile in response to the comparison. The Terran age of thirty-two would be a better estimate for the realm, but of course the man, who'd never stepped through the portal, would fall back on Meridian reckoning.

"I've known you since you were a child," the spokesman continued, "and frankly I'm surprised by what has come to pass."

Instead of the harsh reprimand he'd expected, the man's tone sounded fatherly. He had known Theonis since childhood, many mornings spent in his orchard as they harvested. But, duty was duty, and Cole's thumb twitched as he listened.

"I'm sure I don't need to cite your offenses. You know well the weight of what you have done." Theonis stepped to the edge of the hologram and nodded. "Ignoring the sanctity of life and seeking to end it. Stealing one's freewill by casting a spell denounced by the Gods of Cornerstone Deep. Using the power gifted you to satisfy your unbridled anger..."

Cole closed his eyes as he wished the man had stopped after saying, "You know well the weight of what you have done."

"And knowingly set the noblemen of this plane in a position to pass judgment upon a Sentinel to the Realms."

Yes. Those were the offenses. Every one of them, and it took all his strength not to turn away in shame. Filling his lungs to cleanse his being of the heat in his chest, Cole opened his eyes.

Theonis leaned his head toward Cole and then reached out. His arms extended beyond the edge of the hologram and shimmers filled the opaque limbs. He placed his hands beside Cole's face.

Warmth penetrated Cole's cheeks, so close to a real touch, so close to being connected to home. He blinked in quick succession, and his jaw dropped. *How... How is he...?*

"The Gods know of your soul mate and the part she played in your actions. However, anger and actions must be mastered." He withdrew his touch, and his hands dropped to his sides. "Therefore, you are sanctioned to fill your father's position on Midway Summit."

It was as if frigid air slapped Cole in the face. A myriad of questions flew through his mind, and answers spun twice as fast.

What position of my father's? That of when he saved the travelers? It has to be. I'm to pose as their fake God! So, I'm being reassigned to Midway Summit. What of my duty to Mianna? The decree of one set of Gods are to be upheld by the others! I'm bound to...

His heart sank to his stomach, and he couldn't uphold protocol any longer. He grasped his chest, bunched his shirt into his fist, and doubled over.

My love. My soul mate! Oh, Gods... Mianna.

Chapter Eight

Elaina glanced at Anna as a quirky grin played on her lips. Rhune was the perfect addition to the Shilo family; simply the most stunning member she could have imagined. Next to Anna, or Mianna, as her name and persona turned out to be, he topped the extraordinary. "Do you remember all the things he's talking about? Did Sylis tell you any of this when he was with you?"

Anna's gaze jumped to her and then back to her rings as if she wanted to spend the least amount of time possible to acknowledge the question. "Yes, he spoke of these things."

Okay. "Anna, is something wrong with your rings? You've been staring at them so much this morning."

Mianna tilted the underside of the bands with her thumb. She scooted sideways and flung her leg up to prop her foot on the velvet covered chair beside her. Resting her hands in the dip of her floral print skirt, she leaned her head as if to catch a different view. "Not my wedding band, but the diamond in my engagement ring. It's so odd. Each angle produces a new...vision, something familiar to me that hangs just beyond my grasp. They're like memories." Her brows bit together. "But what do they mean? They're like slivers of images. My life as Mianna is as clear as it could be, at least the part I've lived up to my wedding day to Cole. And that's been four hundred years ago. And the small recollections of Anna's life...it's like I've been thrown into a dream. Like walking a path through the future. But, these...these thoughts, feelings, voices, seem as foreign as if I've stepped into a stranger's mind."

Elaina's exuberance melted as Anna spoke. She knew the experiences her new friend had been through had to be hard to deal with, but she had never opened to Elaina in such a way. She turned to face her fully, and allowed her to share her thoughts.

Anna pressed her lips together, holding the ring steady, and narrowed her eyes. "Come on, Mianna, concentrate. Hold this...whatever it is."

A sigh deflated Anna's shoulders. "If only I could...take just a moment to leave behind all the confusing new developments in my life...and lost lives. You and Linda are my best friends. But you really are strangers to me. And conveniences I'd never dared dream of in the sixteen-hundreds, my true life... If I could just leave it all behind for a few moments, how it would be a welcome change."

Elaina's heart sank. Should she really be the one Anna spoke to about all of this? Perhaps she didn't feel comfortable confessing her true feelings to Cole who would worry and blame himself for the situation all over again.

A glint flashed upward from Anna's ring, and she quickly followed it to the bobble-filled chandelier that hung from the crown of the dining hall. A million sparkles romped among the crystals, free, full of glory within the blue-tinted atmosphere.

Anna stood, staring at the chandelier filled with crystal globes. As if nobody else was in the room, she stepped onto her chair, and then on top of the heavy dining table. Gaze locked on the lights, her hands rose to her sides, and she twirled in a small circle around the centerpiece. "So much that I am! I feel I'm so much more."

Linda appeared at the ingress, accompanied by a trail of smoke from her cigarette. "Have you guys seen...? Anna, what are you...?"

Elaina waved her hand with a shush to quiet her sister. Whatever Anna was experiencing, she obviously needed the moment to be free, not cluttered with Linda's opinions.

Grabbing the coffee pot and sweet rolls from Anna's path, Elaina slid them to the far side of the table.

Anna paused, staring at the sparkling spheres that made up the chandelier. Hanging less than a foot from her face, it illuminated her countenance to shine. The brightest smile Elaina had seen on Anna spread across her cherubic features, and her eyes glistened.

"I see now. I see...mountains of glass, crystal illusions, visions of...home." Anna clasped her hands to her chest and shook her head. "Listen to the singing! Oh, how beautiful it is!" She lifted her hands as if in praise and expelled a large breath with one word. "Oh!"

~ * ~

Vincent slowly lowered his hands to his sides as Cole's face lost all color and then flushed as quickly. He hadn't known what to expect at a Counsel sentencing, but he'd never imagined this. Regardless of how he and Cole felt about each other, they did have one thing in common—a soul mate—

and the worse thing they could have done was separate Cole from his eternal love.

Should I offer a bracing hand, comfort the old brood?

Would it be allowed? He glanced at James for a hint, but the big guy's lips were pressed tight together, and his eyes closed.

Theonis looked to the side and then faced Rhune. As he spoke, Cole seemed to lose his strength and slumped into his chair. He braced his forehead with his fingers and shallow breaths caused his chest to rise and fall in quick, jittery motions.

Brushing the conversation between Theonis and Rhune aside, Vincent marched to Cole and then placed his hand on his shoulder. "Cole," he whispered.

A flood of telepathic information hit Vincent's mind. *"Kid. They're taking me from Mianna. How can they call for this? There must be some mistake. I can't... My heart... I won't survive without..."*

Vincent swallowed and dragged his fingers along the stubble on his chin. He hadn't readied for the day yet, and they delivered such news? Never had this brother opened his heart to him and shared his deep emotions, his fears with him. Sinking to one knee beside the chair, Vincent rested his arm along his thigh.

What could he say? For that matter, would he be allowed to speak?

"You don't have to speak, Kid." The thought came clearly to his mind, and Vincent recalled Cole's enhanced ability to read thoughts as well as share them.

"Cole…"

"My life just ended. I have no purpose without Mianna. I finally got her back, and they're ripping her from me."

Vincent squeezed Cole's shoulder to show support and that he understood the pain he must be feeling. *"Maybe after the position is fulfilled, they'll allow you to return. Midway Summit time will seem very quick to Mianna. It will be like you were gone a week… Or maybe a month at the most."*

Cole shook his head and then glanced at him. *"We're not talking Meridian time. Midway Summit isn't nearly as pronounced."*

"It will still be a fraction of the time… A year, maybe, to your century. And if you're posted near the portal, the time may flow quicker."

A sigh huffed past Cole's parted lips. *"Any time away is too long, Kid."* He placed his hand on Vincent's forearm. *"Thank you, brother. To speak with another about the bond of a soul mate is a gift. I guess we've finally found common ground."*

A smile inched up the corners of Vincent's lips. *"I believe we have."*

Chapter Nine

The atmosphere in the study couldn't get any colder for Rhune as Colhart, Vincentor, and Jamesuranton watched him pace to the window, the hearth, and then to Sylisan's personal role-top desk. He lifted his hand to brush his fingers along the tambour in remembrance of the agreement that led to this moment.

"Don't touch that."

Jamesuranton's voice came through strong as the silencing spell could barely hamper the bark. Rhune pressed his lips together, closed his eyes, and let his hand fall to his side. *It spared our brotherhood, Sylisan, but what will I have to do to save my relationship with Jamesuranton? It's been so long...*

He gazed at his nephews at the front of the room. All eyes stared back, as onyx as the Shilomacj family's ever was. Colhart lounged in his chair, one leg extended, elbows on the armrest, and tapping his finger on his knee. Vincentor had reclaimed his position by the door, arms folded, and leaning on the wall. They could only pass as Sylisan's sons, lean and slender, the corners of their mouths dipped into a natural frown that had often thrown Rhune's judgment of his brother's attitude. While Colhart had acquired his father's talent with telepathy, Vincentor excelled in his mother's gift of light. Though explosives weren't her chosen form of display.

Rhune cocked his eye at the thought, and then shifted his gaze to Jamesuranton. As much as the middle Shilomacj son wanted to deny it, he couldn't hide the fact that he didn't fit Sylisan's mold—in body or talent—and one day, the truth would have to be faced...and accepted.

Vincentor heaved a breath. "Will you just stop your walking and explain what all this is about? I only caught part of what the counsel told you, so as usual, I'm clueless." He drew his hand through the air. "You all know Father didn't bother to share much of the stuff about Midway Summit with me. Well, now it's time to cough it up. What's this prophecy that's been set into play, and what's it got to do with Uncle Rhune and Cole?"

Colhart, folded one leg and stretched the other. "It has nothing to do with me."

"But they're sending you there with Uncle Rhune until it's fulfilled."

"It did have to do with Father, and as

he's not available, and I have the same abilities that he did, I'm called on to fill his position in the trio."

Rhune set his hands at his waist and looked at his feet. "The whole ordeal stemmed from Sylisan's idea. When the group from Cornerstone Summit breached the portal, he saw the opportunity to...fulfill a dream of his. Learn about the people of Earth. He'd always wanted to be assigned there. Had requested several times, but the gods always refused."

Vincentor nodded. "Right. Dressen mentioned that when we confronted him at Shilo Park. He was seeing his past life at the time."

"Well..." Rhune meandered back to the window. "He spoke with Lilith, and after she agreed to help him, he contacted me. I was against it, flat out didn't want to be involved with the matter. Especially with the Counsel fuming that the breach happened at all. As far as I was concerned, the Fountain of Youth seekers could meet their end for trying to outsmart their gods."

"Fountain of Youth?"

"Water that revitalizes life," murmured Colhart.

"Ah." Vincentor's tone held a know-it-all-now air. "So, he laid a guilt trip on you for telling them about it to begin with."

Rhune shook his head. "He offered me a chance at redemption for something that happened before that. The thought of regaining the love and obtaining forgiveness of my only brother drove my involvement in the endeavor."

Slight laughter laced Vincentor's words. "What could you have possibly done that was so bad that Father stopped loving *you*?"

Rhune smiled at the youth's innocence, but he tempered the curve of his lips as he turned and looked at Jamesuranton. "Something I cannot be ashamed of only because of the outcome."

Jamesuranton clenched his teeth and met his gaze.

The grin on Vincentor's face seemed plastered in position as he looked from him, to his large brother, and then back. His arms slowly unfolded and then lowered to his sides, jaw fell slack, and if Rhune read his gaze right, Vincentor's view of him over the past twelve hundred years changed in the flash of his eyes.

Colhart's brows rose as he clasped his hands over his waist, and then he looked at the edge of the cherry-wood desk.

Rhune's assessment of Vincentor's change of perception proved right as a red glow issued from his clenched knuckles.

"You... Mother... James is your *son*?"

Jamesuranton growled his words. "I am not his son."

"You will always be my son, Jamesuranton."

Jamesuranton jumped up, and the master chair wheeled with a spin, ramming into the bookcase behind him.

Colhart quickly stood and stepped between his brothers and Rhune. His telepathic gift punched into Rhune's mind with his retort. *"We're all Shilos! We love, we hate, we fight for what we believe in, and most of all we're always there for each other."* Colhart looked directly at each of them in turn, and then held his hands out at his sides. "Especially when times are hard. And right now, times couldn't get much harder. We need to put aside what happened over a millennium ago."

Rhune swiped his finger across his nose as a flood of appreciation calmed his heart. He knew Colhart's view on the matter, they didn't see things the same on many fronts. But Colhart's show of support, considering the task he'd been assigned, was gallant on his part.

"Even if we're reminded of it every time we look at Rhune," added Colhart in a low voice, as if he'd read Rhune's thoughts and felt he had to clarify his stand.

Rhune turned his head and aimlessly scanned the magical trinkets on the mantel. What was he thinking? Of course, he'd read his thoughts.

Colhart set his fists at his belt as he shifted his weight. "What matters right now is that we complete our mission. Now. James. I can't believe I'm saying this, because frankly, you've always been the rational one. But are you ready to take on the responsibility of Head Sentinel and lead without letting your personal issues get the better of you? Because Kid would be next in line to satisfy the call. And I would have issues with that."

A slight sneer quirked the corner of Vincentor's lips, but it disappeared as he looked at his large brother.

Jamesuranton straightened and placed his fingertips on the desktop. "Rhune what do you know of this prophecy the Counsel spoke of?"

As Colhart reclaimed his seat, Rhune filled his lungs and lifted his chin. So much had happened recently to destroy the boys' memories of their father. Could he go through with adding yet another chapter to the book of selfish deeds? Then, what choice did he have? "There was one among the settlers who was said to be a sensitive to the spirits. When she received the Gift of

Life, her talent was enhanced. She spoke of many prophecies and her scribe recorded them for posterity.

"One concerned the Allants...the name we were christened, which means High Ones. Many of the people deemed us gods and feared it would bring our wrath upon them if it was kept, so they buried it deep in a mountainside. Of course, we knew what it said, the Counsel does have its ways, does it not?"

He held up his hand and set an aimless walk around the room. "It spoke of how we, the High Ones, offered life, light, and knowledge to the displaced souls from Earth. How they were gifts that blessed them as they sought a new life among the folds of Moraine. But it pointed out that there was one who led a tribe that made a covenant with Knowledge—that would be Sylisan—to keep his line pure. A creed of valiance was to follow them until which time Knowledge would return and be monarch."

A red glow grew around Vincentor's fists. "He wanted to rule over these people?"

Rhune stepped into a turn. He was right; another bad chapter to the seemingly endless ruthless acts performed by his brother. He didn't need to see the result of his nephew's anger.

"The covenant line of settlers journeyed beneath the crust of the planet. They took with them a line of natives who swore to uphold the pledge and offer aid. They live deep in the caverns of Moraine to this day.

"But the gods love their children, do they not? And where acts affect natural eternal progression, they intervene. It's one law my dear brother simply could not understand fully." He faced his nephews and set his hands at his waist. "The prophecy speaks of a slave with gifts who will serve with meekness and seek to please. He will be favored and rise quickly in the status of slavery. It is said, 'He is Allant. He is Knowledge.'"

Vincentor held up his hand as he faced Jamesuranton. "Wait. Didn't you say they named Father Allant when he was reborn?"

Jamesuranton heaved a sign and nodded as he closed his eyes.

"So, you're telling me this prophetess told everyone that Father would be reborn as a slave? That's what you said, 'He is Allant. He is Knowledge.'"

Rhune squelched his cheek. "That's right, my boy. However, few heard of that part of the prophecy. It was hidden long before the information leaked to very many ears. The prophecy also tells of a visionary among those who master, born of the Gift of Knowledge. These gifts were inherent, as it turned out, from others who opted to follow the clan after receiving the gift."

Colhart craned his neck, looking at Rhune behind him. "Are you telling me there are people on Midway Summit that have the same abilities we do?"

"Not the same, Colhart. Only a small glimpse of the possibilities. Many have no idea where their talents come from, though a birthmark identifies these souls as sons or daughters of the tribal leaders who were blessed."

"Proceed," said Jamesuranton without making eye contact.

With a nod, Rhune continued. "The prophecy also foretells of a time when Light, Life, and Knowledge shall return, bringing with them an Angel of Love who shall know Allant and aid in his decisive act that will hold the fate of nations in the balance." He let his hand waver through the air. "There's more but I believe this will suffice for now."

Silence held Rhune's words suspended as the three, no doubt, contemplated the information. Jamesuranton's lips pressed into a tight line, Vincentor flexed his glowing fingers, and Colhart's head eased back onto the chair's cushion. Could any of them truly understand the magnitude of what lay before them?

Jamesuranton nodded and placed his palms down on the desk. "As the gods have called for the Allants to gather and fulfill the prophecy, Rhune shall stand in for himself as the God of Life. Cole shall take the place of Father as the God of Knowledge, and Vincent shall fill in for Mother as the God of Light. The Angel of Love of whom the prophecy foretells will join you when she or he is revealed to us."

Rhune rolled his jaw and prepared for an explosion. "Vincentor is not needed in regard to the prophecy. Lilith's soul is available and the purest talent. She merely needs to be trained. The Counsel has not called on him to take her place."

His son's nostrils flared, chest expanded, and nails scraped along the top of the desk as he bunched his fingers into fists. Colhart and Vincentor cringed in unison as they closed their eyes.

Rhune lifted his chin and placed the crooks of his thumbs at his waist. His son may be centuries younger, more limber, and—dare he say—had a wee bit more muscle on him, but he had the upper hand when it came to manipulate the elements. Something can be said for years of experience, and no one was going to come between Mechenzie and her destiny.

Jamesuranton spoke through clenched

teeth. "*Coneko silyst.*"

The silencing spell released the room and morning bird chirps sounded from beyond the window. Jamesuranton tossed his hand out to his side, and Rhune flinched as the door flung wide. His son marched out, and Vincentor turned on his heel, following. Colhart leaned into his stride and then strode out behind them.

A long stream of air left Rhune's lungs as he dragged his palm down his face. The last thing he wanted was a confrontation with his son. Heavens, he wanted to win the boy's approval. What was it like all those years for Sylisan, to have Jamesuranton look at him with hero worship in his eyes? Rhune could count many times he'd walked in on the two, only to have Sylisan look up to see him as Jamesuranton peered at the man with such a look. He'd read smugness in each instance.

And who could blame him?

To pursue a woman in wedlock was one of the most disgraceful things a man could do, soul mate or not. One waited. The next life could be spent in search of her. With the bond securely around her soul, she would wait or join in the search. He'd crossed one of the largest lines there could be between Meridian brothers.

But, Rhune had to wonder. Vincentor's

soul, now living his first lifespan, had to be created to fill this Sentinel family's promise of three to keep the triad alive. As offspring are assigned to their sires, Rhune was destined to be Jamesuranton's father. What if he hadn't seduced Lilith? Would they birth yet another new soul for the family, and leave it with two inexperienced youngsters?

Swiping his finger across his nose, Rhune sniffed. "Ah, I'm just seeking justification, am I not?"

"I don't know. Are you?"

With a start, Rhune faced the door, and Linda placed her hand on a very voluptuous hip. "Seen my lover?"

"You just missed him, my Terran flower."

"Why do you do that?"

"Do what, love?"

"Have to give everyone pet names? Elaina and Anna told me about it. I wondered what you'd come up with for me."

"Ah, well, you see, I don't have to. It's just a kind gesture I learned long ago, while on Cornerstone Summit. They called their loves flower, pet, angel, honey, darling... The list was endless. And I'd come to find I quite like the sentiment."

"Huh. Well, my name is Linda."

Rhune offered a slight bow. "My

apologies, Leenja, if I've offended you."

"Don't call me that either."

"But I thought you said it was your name."

"It is, but only James says it like that."

Rhune tilted his head. "Like what?"

"Like Leenja."

"How would you have me pronounce it?"

"Linda."

Rhune pursed his lips into an exaggerated try. "Leenja."

"No, Linda."

"Lenja."

"Linda!"

"Len-ja."

The back and forth play with the name as he attempted to say it right almost bubbled into laughter as he tried once more. "Len-za!"

Clenching her hands into fists, exasperation exploded from her like a roar. "Augh!"

Rhune shrugged, hands lifting to his sides as he upped his brow. She turned and stormed out of the room.

His humor stumbled from his gut in short chuckles. "Ah, Linda. You are a fierce Terran woman. Perhaps you should be called Tiger Lily."

Shilo Manor series~Destiny

Chapter Ten

Each step Cole took seemed automatic as he trailed the hallway to his room. Pastels hung in his side vision and cast the faint sense of cinnamon crumb cake to his senses; an odd observation that contrasted heavily with the outcome of his sentence. He blinked as his thoughts jumbled next to the thick pulse in his temples. Sandpaper coated the back of his throat. He swallowed, forcing his Adam's apple to bob. It squelched.

He'd spent the last four hundred years without his true love, the only woman to see beneath the fronts he often played, and now that he had her back in his life the Gods deemed it necessary to separate them. How cruel a joke. How heartless and ungodlike the decision. Cole gnawed on his bottom lip as he neared their room. He'd broken both law and covenant. He deserved punishment. How selfish he was being in the grand scheme of things, but he couldn't help it.

How long would he have with her before the Council directed him to Midway Summit? Wasn't he to serve her for the rest of his soul's existence, watch over her, and protect her? How in the name of the Spectrum could he do that from another plane? It didn't make sense. The Council acted as messengers, passing on the judgment of the Gods of Meridian. Yet, honoring the discipline set by another set of Gods was among the highest of ethereal laws. He clenched his jaw and attempted to set thoughts of his new calling aside.

As he reached for the door latch, a soft voice penetrated the troubles in his mind. Leaning close, he listened carefully, as if being nearer would bring the telepathic conversation clearer to him. Another feminine voice joined in, and he tilted his head to decipher the meaning. Perhaps it wasn't telepathic, and Mianna had someone with her?

He quietly opened the door a crack.

Mianna sat on the bed, peering at the diamond ring in her wedding set, and he realized he indeed heard the other person from her thoughts. But something seemed off. It wasn't in Mianna's voice, as if she was remembering a past conversation. Surrounding sounds came to him with clarity, and as he focused more fully, crisp details took shape in his mind.

A woman's eyes twinkled as she smiled from beside a fruit stand. Her portly figure filled the brown and white folds of her dress, and Cole associated the style to that of the seventeenth century. Heavy clip-clops sounded in the distance and cemented his assessment. But why would this be in Mianna's thoughts, so clear, so...real?

A white gloved hand reached away from Cole, as if he were the person in the vision, seen through his eyes. The woman handed him a basket of fruit. "Will that be all, Miss Airabelle?"

Mianna answered aloud, posing as Airabelle in the experience. "I believe these will make a perfect setting, Mrs. Curtis." *She handed the woman five coins and then looped the basket handle in the crook of her burgundy, lace-adorned elbow.*

With a grin, Mrs. Curtis slipped the money into her skirt pocket. "Sir William is sure to be pleased."

Tilting her head, Mianna narrowed her eyes. "And what do you know of Sir William?"

The woman's ample breasts shook as she chortled. "Oh, only that he fancies you beyond any other maiden in the city. You do make a handsome couple."

"William and I are merely friends."

Cole shook his head as he watched what would appear to anyone else as a one-sided conversation. But Mianna stared at the shiny gem with such depth; he knew she believed it to be as real as him standing at the door watching her.

Mrs. Curtis wobbled a stubby finger in Airabelle's direction. "Now, now, Miss Gifford," she said in a quiet voice. "You face spinsterhood if you keep turning young men away."

"Spinsterhood will be a welcome arrival if my soul mate does not find me by then. And so will my senescent years."

Her soul mate?

"You spend too much time among the old," said Mrs. Curtis. "You should leave that geriatric home and enjoy life. Besides, Sir William Burton could be that soul mate idea you cling to so."

William Burton... Cole filed through his memory to pinpoint the name. His jaw dropped. *That's Father's name from one of his lifetimes. This is more than a memory; she's reliving a moment in a previous life!*

How could that be? He'd anointed the ring with no memories, no charm to enhance focus or recall the past. In every way, the token of his proposal was simply that.

Mianna set her hand on her hip and tilted her head. "He's spoken to you, hasn't he? He told me that exact same thing just last week."

The lady's lips pursed into a little O. "So what if he did? I didn't know Martin would fill my heart so fully until we'd spent years together. A love grows stronger with time. You'll discover that you and William will be the same. You just don't realize it yet."

"Mm-hmm. And what you don't realize is that I don't recognize him as my soul mate, because he's not my soul mate. But he's out there." Mianna winked. "I'll know it when he looks into the windows of my soul."

Warmth washed over Cole's heart, and a smile spread his lips. He crossed the ingress and waved the door closed with his finger. The thick carpet hushed his steps as he rounded the bed. Sinking to one knee before her, he ignored the fact that she didn't acknowledge his presence. "My love, may the windows of your soul always search for mine alone."

Mianna's lips parted, and her lashes batted as if she couldn't believe her eyes. She met his gaze, released a quick breath, and then swallowed so hard she gasped. "Cole." Tears misted her beautiful blue gaze. "I've waited so long. So long. I remember...so many times I turned down those who would court me."

Her fist clutched the ring on her finger as if it held the moment in its golden surface, and she refused to let go. "Arylin promised you would find me again...that your soul cried to find mine. And I believed her with my whole heart."

Cole wrapped her hands with his palms. "So it was, Mianna, and so it is even now. My soul longs for you every waking moment."

The sun peeked through the window, and sparks danced off the diamond in her ring as she slid her hands from beneath his. Wrapping her arms around his neck, she pulled him into a tender kiss. He embraced the most treasured soul in his life and closed his eyes.

Mianna.

Pure love poured from her, complete, unquestioning, and Cole's soul ached. Whenever they deemed it time to fulfill the prophecy would be too soon.

Mianna's soft voice interrupted Cole's thoughts and called him back to the precious moment. Her hand lifted from his shoulder as she looked at the ring. "I've remembered things the last couple days."

"My love, perhaps when Unsigh carried you back to Mianna's life, your mind was opened to your other experiences that would aid in your soul's progression.

She shook her head, patience evident in her loving voice. "It's beyond Unsigh. I believe Arylin is speaking to me, showing me important moments from my lives. And I think it's time that I read the book."

His furrowed his brow. "What book?"

She pulled away enough to look into his eyes. "The book the gods gave your father when I was to be born."

"The gods gave Father a book when you were born?"

"Not when I was born. When I was to be born. I know it sounds absurd, Cole. But I saw it. Arylin handed it to him."

"Your life as Mianna was your first, my love. You wouldn't see the happenings of things before then. The gods have to birth a new soul at that time."

Mianna blinked, and her thumb ran across the bottom of her rings. Her head slowly moved from side to side. "I saw it," she whispered.

Rocking backward on his knee, Cole braced himself against the sinking sensation in his stomach. Through the emotions he picked up from her, he knew she believed what she saw to be truth with every fiber of her being, and with it entailing his father, whatever would come of this could not be good.

Chapter Eleven

Vincent splashed water on his face, and then wiped it along his hair. The cool refreshment elicited the shudder that had edged him from the time he left the study. The story of the prophecy only pushed the memories of his father further into a bog he didn't want to visit. How could one man accomplish so much deceit in his lifetime?

And to the point of changing the natural course of evolution for an entire world? "Thank the Gods I wasn't in on everything that happened," he murmured. "This is enough to carry through the next thousand years."

"Vince?" Elaina's voice filtered to him from the bedroom, and his soul welcomed the sweet sound.

"In here."

Strawberry curls appeared around the door, followed by the most beautiful red-head in Shilo City. He swiped a towel over his face, tossed it in the sink, and then turned to take her in his arms. The charming mouth that spoke his name curved upward as he pulled her tightly against him and then stepped into a circle. Her laughter wrapped around his heart, warmed his chest with joy, and as he drank in the pure sunshine in her freckled countenance, his worries drifted to the back of his mind.

Elaina.

How could he be so lucky, so blessed to have found the soul in his first lifespan who would accompany him through the eternities? He bent to taste her lips, but his jaw slowly dropped as the reality of his thoughts washed over him. So few found their true soul mate before two lifetimes passed, yet the gods had guided them together. A small grin played on his lips as he recalled how they first met.

He hadn't been keen on attending the opening of Vissoni's Art Fountain that day with James, but something urged him to go. As he walked around a three-tiered waterfall, she came into view like an artist's rendition of a fairy tale princess. The only thing taming the curls of her long strawberry blonde hair was a bow pinned high on the crown of her head. The rest tumbled down her back in bunched waves of unrestrained charm. Her profile painted the epitome of innocence: a gentle slope that ended in a little upturned nose, light brown freckles that dotted the cutest apple cheeks he'd seen, and blue eyes that sparkled as she peered at the magical-

Charlene A. Wilson

looking shapes produced by the streams of water within the artist's instrument. The daughter of the owner of the largest pool of artisans in the city seemed to tear her gaze from the wonderment to look his way...

Vincent's palate tingled as the scent of honey mixed with the natural licorice aroma of the men of Meridian. The Breath of Zypher swirled around his tongue, and he allowed it to pool against his love's face to manifest his desire.

Elaina's hands traveled his back and then gripped his shoulders as he tangled his fingers into her curls. "Elaina. My home."

Her voice came forth in an airy breath. "Vince. You seem so intense. Is everything okay?"

He shook his head. *If you only knew.* "If I could just forget, for a while, that I'm a Sentinel whose duty is to the Gods and must be fulfilled at any cost."

Her perplexed gaze melted, and she seemed to search for something within him. "Oh, Vincent. If only I could take your cares away."

Vincent sucked a stream of air through his teeth. "If I had my way, I would take you to the furthest reaches of Terra and spend eternity making love to you. I need you so much right now."

"Remember the time you rushed me upstairs by Smoke of Night after you learned about what your father did? I felt how much you needed me and never experienced anything like that before. I felt your pain. Your heart was open to me in a way no one else has ever been in my life. Do it now, Vince. Take on the Smoke of Night with me in your arms. Allow me to share your troubles."

Vincent leaned his head in wonder. Such love to want to take on his worries in that way. It was true; disembodiment multiplied the senses and made it hard to hide feelings from someone. But her asking for the experience solidified their everlasting commitment to love. "Oh, Elaina."

"Do it, Vince," she whispered. A quick breath puffed against his lips, and she wriggled in his embrace. "Fly with me into the heights, and make love to me with your everything."

He had to admit that was one thing he'd never experienced—or thought about for that matter. Forget his cares. Forget his new position and the prophecy. To share his innermost feelings with Elaina would be so appropriate...and blasted *hot*! A low growl rumbled in his throat.

Vincent peered at the beautiful windows of her soul. His fingertips skimmed her shoulders, and the straps to her sundress slid down her arms. Savoring the soft skin at her neck, he dissolved their bodies into the Smoke of Night.

A wash of excitement burst from her as their disembodiment freed thought and heart. Every fiber of her opened to him, trusting, subjective. Never had he been given the gift of total access to all corners of a woman's being: Love, fear, insecurities, rage...and with Elaina, it was so damned erotic!

Vincent whisked them high into the upper scope of their bedroom. Talking about it held nothing to experiencing it first hand, and the small embers that ignited in the lavatory burst into flares. Heat pulsed within their dark cloud with each swoop, turn, and trill they rode. Cool air filtered through the open window and felt like an icy blast against their aroused essences.

His heart exploded—or was it another part of him? Who cared? Eternity stretched in all directions, and Elaina accompanied him in a seductive dance of love.

Elaina's particles shivered in conjunction with her thoughts of his touch, and he turned her higher, pressing the moment to allow her the most of the experience. He imagined her deep breath lifting two perfect breasts, the arch in her cloud as her back against the blanket.

His excitement escalated, throwing bright glittering power sparks to dance within their essences.

She ebbed from him, swooped to the edge of his reach, and then merged with him, pressing against particles he didn't know existed.

Delirium sent his mind in a whirl.

Spangles erupted from deep within their joined particles. Each movement ground against his will, and a fire he didn't know existed within her burned him from inside out.

Strobes flashed. Flares arched in all directions, and as he tightened their molecules to push the pleasure to its fullest, bulbs in the chandelier exploded. Sprites of electricity glistened through their cloud.

Oh, holy ethereal Gods!

Vincent grabbed at Elaina's essence, spun around the burst electrical outlets, and then pulled their particles together, letting their clothes land on the floor. As they formed on the downy comforters, their bodies still joined, he released the roar once silenced by disembodiment. Hot air hit his chest in wild puffs, unhindered growls riding her breathing. Her nails dug into his skin as she dragged them down his back, and he didn't think her legs could wrap around him any tighter.

Spasms of fire jolted his body, and he never wanted it to end. He braced her shoulders and ground into her, intent on filling every inch.

Her husky cry flew through him in a rush, and he pressed harder. "Vincent!"

In a flash, the coil within him burst, and he growled his victory to the heavens. She joined in with guttural sounds, and Vincent understood all too well. He'd never experienced such fulfilment of love, openness, and acceptance.

Panting beside her ear, Vincent shook his head in disbelief. He had Elaina, his soul mate, his home. And for the first time in his life, he felt the weight and the freedom in such a blessing. "Gods, Elaina. I love you."

He gazed at the amazing woman beneath him. Her hair, a mess of matted nets, tickled his face, and he kissed the beautiful sight.

The most wonderful woman in the Arched Spectrum of Realms lifted her hooded gaze to his. "And Gods, I love you, Vincent."

Shilo Manor series~Destiny

Chapter Twelve

The white blossom trees along the hillside passed in a haze as Rhune flew toward the edge of town. Contraptions rambled on the black-topped streets, emitting obnoxious fumes. Terrans walking on the waysides didn't seem to notice but combined with the events that had just taken place, all he wanted to do was heave.

Dipping into a narrow alley, he found the shadows and then left behind Smoke of Night travel. His back hit the brick wall as he expelled a deep breath and closed his eyes.

Colhart will stand in as the God of Knowledge. Well, now, won't that be a joy? And a little girl must mature and be trained to accomplish the task she began in her previous life as Lilith. He let his head fall to the side. *But only after I manage to get her away from her fiery Terran mother and my only son who shoots venom at me with a simple look.*

A low growl rumbled in his throat. "Sylisan, if I didn't know better, I'd swear you'd planned things to end up this way all along."

He swiped his finger across his nose. *Lilith will have to return to Meridian to be ready to face the lesser realms as a fully groomed enchantress in time, and that would leave Colhart to remove the manor on Midway Summit from shadow. You and I both know he lacks in intricate manipulation.*

Rhune's vivid imagination conjured the perfect pitch for Sylisan to speak to his mind—a brotherly bark, as he rustled his hair, that grew tender with small rises and falls in the tempo as the answer entered Rhune's thoughts.

"Regardless of Jamesuranton's view of you, Rhuen-it, he will follow the Gods' instructions to a tee, no matter how it will pain him to do so. Colhart will come through for you, though he might drag his feet and mope around. And Lilith will be at your side, fighting to fulfill all that is to come to pass."

Rhune chuckled as he recalled the old nickname, and then his smile faded. He'd never hear it again. Unless, of course, he visited more imaginary voices from the past.

With a nod, Rhune leaned away from the wall, shifted his neck to the side until it popped, and then stretched his shoulders. Gathering his wits, he stepped from the alley and followed the little storefronts that lined the street. Shabby and gray, they brought back memories of his time in a similar realm; one whose inhabitants had started the whole mess he faced.

Twin pots of yellow and pink flowers decorated the stoop of Pappy's Pub in invitation to passers-by. "I like the place for the name alone," he said to no one in particular. "But the flowers cinch it for me."

Rhune skipped up the steps and entered. The old eatery couldn't have been wider than thirty feet but looked three times as deep. Small round tables pocked the front end with what appeared to be original paintings lining the white walls. A narrow stage sat midway down the structure, and he tapped his fingers along the keyboard of a piano that had seen better days. The tinkle of tones broke the silence of the nearly empty space.

A man leaned to the side, peering around his shoulder from a table near the bar in the back. "Charlotte, looks like you got an early bird."

Rhune tugged out a chair and sat as a woman walked from a door behind the counter.

"Well, aren't we up and at it with the sun this morning." She smiled, and her hand flicked to signify her other customer. "Let me get Jarrett here his beer. I'll be right with you."

Rhune glanced at Jarrett and cocked his brow. Four bottles already stood in front of the man. In fact, he looked as if he'd been there all night. Blond streaked hair fell over his eyes and stubble shadowed his jawline. The tailored suit he wore was wrinkled. As he leaned back and flung his arm over the back of his chair, Rhune noticed the shirt had been unbuttoned three deep, and the tie hung like a loose noose.

Charlotte placed another beer beside the four empty bottles, and Jarrett tossed a bundle of currency onto her tray. She tilted her head, causing her brown curls to tumble off her shoulder. "Pick up that money, Jarrett."

He took her free hand in his grip and palm-walked his way up her arm. "I'm not here to pick up money." He rose, following the climb to her neck, and stepped behind her, gently messaging her shoulders. "When do you get off, beautiful?"

She looked at Rhune with a smirk. "Always the same bundle of money, the same climb, the same question. Why don't I call you a cab, bad boy?"

Jarrett buried his face in her thick curls and hummed.

Rolling her eyes, she lightly thumped

him on the head with her tray and then leaned to call around him. "Pappy, Jarrett's finally ready to go home."

A voice came from a distance, and the tenor did indeed sound like it came from a dear old pappy. "A'right, doll."

With a groan, Jarrett flumped back into his chair. "Don't wanna go home. Don't want to even know it's there. Let me just stay here, Char. You keep me in beer; I'll keep you in business."

"Your liver will dissolve before I run out of beer," she murmured as she stepped to Rhune's side.

"Sandra's gone," grumbled Jarrett into the lip of his beer bottle.

Footsteps shuffled from behind the bar, and by the look of the man, he could only be Pappy. Kinky salt and pepper hair sprinkled the crown of his head and gave way to a tall brow. Crinkles edged the twinkle in his eyes as he looked at Jarrett and nodded. "For a man who lives the noble life, you look like hell, son."

"Linda's gone."

"Yes, I know." The elder looped the inebriated soul's arm around his shoulder. "Up we go."

"And my golden girls are up there on that hill with a Founder who has arms the size of...tree trunks." His head lulled to the side as he looked at Rhune. "Like his."

Pappy chuckled and grabbed Jarrett's suit jacket from the back of his chair. "The car's in the back. Let's get you to that nice house of yours."

As the two shuffled out, Charlotte turned to Rhune. "I haven't seen you around here. Were you in town for that grand gathering of the faithful?"

He shook his head and held up his index finger. "Extenuating circumstance. But it was indeed a grand gathering, was it not? I understand the Lord Marshall has passed on to his next life. I take it he will be missed by many?"

Charlotte's cheek quirked against her heart-shaped face, and her head tilted. "Lord Marshall? You really aren't from around here, are you?"

A chuckle rode his words. "Oh, my home is very far away."

"He was the Senior Grand Marshal, and I don't know how well he was liked, but his memorial is tomorrow. You planning to settle here in Shilo?"

"No, my visit won't be for long." He reached into his shirt pocket and pinched the tip of one of his D-Lotuses. The long straw-like stem materialized as he withdrew it. As he nipped the end, a silver mist pooled around his lips, and serenity blanketed his mind. Concerns of his new assignment, and the conversation that had followed the news, melted to mere happenings. "Much to the joy of my hosts, I should say."

He chuckled as he leaned back in his chair and then peered at the beauty before him.

Charlotte's eyes grew wide as she focused on the mist before Rhune's face. Her chin trembled. "You're one of them. A Founder, aren't you?" Her nose flared as her words tumbled forth. "They're the only ones who have trinkets like that. I know firsthand. I thought I was crazy, until all that happened at Shilo Park with Lord Dressen, and they revealed their true identities." Something between a scoff and a snort sounded in her throat. "And to think someone from some grand place appointed by the Gods would honestly want a lasting relationship with me. No wonder Tom was always so vague."

Rhune glanced at his D-Lotus and grimaced. When would he learn to be more careful in foreign dimensions? "I do apologize. I didn't mean to startle you." He lifted the slender instrument for her to view. "I brought this from my home. It's a Lotus. Produces a fine mist that coats the sensitive tissues of the mouth and affects the pleasure senses in the brain." His chest shook with his low chortle. "It allows me to relax without the repercussions our friend Jarrett experiences from the drink."

She eyed the thing, and then her gaze met his. "I've never heard of it. Are you saying you're not a Founder and they make these things somewhere on Terra?"

"Oh, I'm not a Founder, but they are my nephews. And I must say, I don't believe any of them are named Tom, Sh'létte."

A quick breath left her lips, and she lightly placed her hands to her heart as she sat in an empty chair. Her words came out as barely a breath. "Oh, Gods. He used to call me that. Sh'létte. I thought he chose to say my name in a special way, but it's part of your accent?"

"Ah. Then you must be speaking of Colhart. As long as he's served here, he still hasn't quite lost the lilt of our native tongue."

Moisture glazed her chocolate eyes. "Colhart? His name isn't Cole either?"

"Yes, my Terran charm, he's known as Cole here. Just a shortened nickname, as when Jarrett called you Char earlier. Nothing more."

Charlotte blinked the beads of tears from her lashes, and Rhune leaned forward, reaching along the table. He gently placed his palm over her hand. "And if it's Colhart of whom you speak, you have every right to believe he was looking for a lasting relationship. Especially if you dated for a significant amount of time."

"Almost four months," she whispered.

"Well, then. I'd say you are a special one. Last I heard, if Colhart couldn't connect with a woman on a soul mate level, he would—"

"End it."

Rhune nodded. "Something kept him with you. He wanted it to be you."

"He kept saying... 'Speak to me,' he would say, 'Speak to me with your soul.'" A sob punched from her lips, and her fists beat her thighs. "How do you make your soul say anything? Isn't it who we are? Don't we talk every day? Is there a special word I don't know about? Because I tried to pour my entire heart out to him, told him I loved him, showed him how much I cared... What else is there?"

The plea in sweet little Charm's wet eyes wrapped his heart in a knot. Oh, these young realms, so lost in their search for love. So blind to the eternal connection available to them to understand several millennia could pass in a quick crinkling of Pappy's lids.

Rhune placed his D-Lotus aside and

took her hands in his. "He looked for a soul mate's call, my little Terran charm. He wanted your soul to reach out to his, as if the arms of your spirit would wrap around him and penetrate every fiber of his being." He leaned his head to the side. "You don't understand this. Your dimension is so much younger than the one our family comes from."

She inched her hands from beneath his. "Did you say dimension?"

There I go again. He brushed the query aside as he tucked a few straggling curls behind her ear. "He loved you very much, but alas, he found his soul mate, lost nearly four hundred years ago. They reunited to continue their lives together, and their souls' progressions."

Charlotte seemed unable to speak. Her jaw dropped, and her fists wrapped tightly around her upper arms. A small whisper passed her lips. "How can I fight a spirit for the man I love?"

"I'm not gifted to see the outcome of one's life, but I can say with all confidence that you, Sh'létte, will find a man who will fill your heart to overflowing."

Caramel curls hid her face as she lowered her head, and Rhune stood. Holding out his fingers, a bundle of bills lighted in his grasp from his pocket. "As my time is spent, I must be going. I'm not familiar with the currency value here. So many different trades on each plane, I find it impossible to keep up." He set five colorful ones on the table. As he reached for his Lotus, he paused. With a glance at the sad little Terran woman, he left it where it lay and turned to leave. She, no doubt, needed it more than he did. "Thank you for keeping this old traveler company in a strange town."

Grasping the edge of Jamesuranton's cloak, he furled the panel and took on the Smoke of Night.

Charlotte's eyes flew wide again, and her chair scrapped across the floor as she darted for the bar.

There you go again, Rhune. Mentally kicking himself, he flew out of Pappy's Pub and into the sunny day. *When will you ever learn to use your head?*

Shilo Manor series~Destiny

Chapter Thirteen

Cardboard boxes flew through the room and smashed into the far-left wall of the basement. James marched to them and kicked aside random items that had scattered across the floor. Every novelty Rhune had sent Vincent from the time they left Meridian to settle in Cornerstone Deep seemed present...except for the one he sought.

Clenching his fists, he forced himself to turn away without crushing them, but then looked back.

Cole's voice came from the basement lab on the other side of the divider. "You could crush them for the satisfaction, and then reassemble. Just a thought."

Despite his disgruntlement, a grin cracked James' scowl. *I could...*

He peeked around the wide wall that separated the two rooms. "What are you doing in the lab?"

"Trying to smooth out an after-effect of a mistake. Dressen's sister, Kendra, has always been a gracious woman. I plan on presenting her with a gift."

James eyed the tools laid out on the table before Cole: The family's Candle

Vignette, displaying instructions in its flame, bowls, spices... "And you're using the memory box for this? Cole, we don't need a repeat of what happened."

Cole shook his head as a soft mist fell from his hand to the center of a bowl. "A gift for her own enjoyment, to remember only the good of her brother. Surely she has fond memories of him at some point in her life."

He straightened and looked at James, a twinge scrunching the left side of his face. "I can't let my doing be the cause of her callous memories of him."

"Ah, I see." James turned and rummaged through another box.

"And what has you so up in arms over there?"

"Looking for something."

"Okay. What?"

"The picture Mother took of me sitting on Father's knee."

A sound much like a scoff came from Cole's side of the room. "That wouldn't be in boxes of Vincent's gifts from Rhune."

James paused and furrowed his brow. "How did you know I..." He caught himself and shook his head. Of course, Cole read his heated thoughts when he found and threw the memorabilia. "Never mind."

"Let it go, James."

James set his hands at his waist. "I

can't. I can't stand the man. I cringe every time he calls me son."

Footsteps creaked on the wooden staircase behind him, and Linda's voice broke into his irritation.

"I see you're redecorating down here."

James swiveled on his heal to see her arms crossed, hip leaning on the plank banister. Little white shoes hopped down the steps, and then the rest of the twins appeared as they descended.

Mandy squealed with a little gasp and darted for the odds-n-ends scattered among the broken cardboard. "Wow, Poppa James, where did you get all of these?"

Light shimmered off the silver and gold curios, making the memorabilia a joy-land for any child.

He wiped his palm over his head. "Looking for something and ran across them."

Mechenzie rushed behind him. "What's in this?"

As he turned, Linda stepped to his side and lifted the booklet-sized package from her grip. "Kenzie, you know better than to touch."

"But it's glowing."

James took it from Linda's hand. A simple twine held parchment tightly wrapped around it, and a mute light indeed filtered through the thick paper. A magical item stored in the basement? He turned it over, studying the bundle. *How did this get here?*

Linda's fingers lighted on his bicep. "James, what's wrong? You look like you've seen a ghost."

"I've organized every box and package of this room."

Her blonde brows arched, and she pointedly blinked. "Are you going to expound on that?"

"I don't recognize this. And I highly doubt, with it emitting light, it should be in a storage room."

"Honey? I know you guys do super sensitive nobody-can-know type stuff, but seriously, you're scaring me. I've only known you for a short time, but you don't seem like the type to act...like you've been acting since your uncle showed up."

With a heavy sigh, James nodded. "You're right, Leenja. I haven't been myself."

He looked at the beautiful woman who'd taken hold of his heart. Perhaps it was time to fill the Terran mother of his Meridian mother's soul in on what could be the worst nightmare of her life.

He stroked Mechenzie's cheek with his finger, and then thumbed toward the scattered trinkets. "Why don't you girls pick something out to play with from your Uncle Vincent's toys and then come with us? We all need to have a meeting with the other grown-ups."

Linda's head leaned to the side as Mechenzie ran to Mandy. Squeals and giggles filled the large enclosure as they gathered treasures from the floor.

Ignoring Linda's gaze that said, *what in the name of Gryffin is all this about*, James clutched the package and trotted up the steps to the foyer hallway. What needed said might affect everyone in the household.

~ * ~

Elaina's fingers tapped her knees in quick succession, and Vincent leaned toward her, placing his hand over the nervous motion. "Relax. It's just a meeting."

Her toes took over the quick movement, and a rush of air blew through her lips. "I know," she whispered.

"Then what's wrong?"

"I'm just..." She arched her shoulders, and the tempo in her feet pushed her knees to bounce. "I don't know. I've had so much energy since we...you know."

With a chuckle, he edged closer to her

ear and then placed kisses along her neck. "That was the most phenomenal love making of my life."

Her freckled complexion blushed, and a smile bloomed on her lips. "Me too."

Cole leaned away from Mianna at his side to within an inch of Vincent and gave him a wry smile. He whispered into his ear. "Now that I've got to try."

In a flash, Vince grabbed the old brood's collar in his fist and pulled him close. Forget the brotherly bond from earlier, this topic was off limits. The hiss in his words portrayed the instant anger he wanted to get across. "You keep those mindreading talents in check or I'll blow off a part of you you'll miss the rest of your years."

Cole motioned to Vincent's hand over Elaina's palm. "I merely meant that I needed to try holding Mianna's hands when she starts to fidget from nervousness." He quirked an eye. "What were you referring to?"

Right. Vincent released his brother as James sat at the master chair. Linda stood at his side.

Elaina's hand broke free of Vincent's hold, and she patted the armrests as she turned and looked at Mandy and Mechenzie playing tea by the window. "I think I'll just go join them, Vince. I can

128

listen from there."

As he opened his mouth to respond, she slid from the chair and scampered to the girls like a critter. They giggled, and she laughed as she ended her caper with a romp.

To Vincent's relief, James spoke as if he hadn't noticed the antics. It would have been impossible to keep Elaina pinned down at the moment, and Vincent was glad for the girl's sideshow to keep her fidgeting satisfied. He faced the Head Sentinel mid-sentence.

"Seeing as the entire crew is here for this, I see no need to seal the room in silence. Any of you disagree?"

Vincent glanced around the room. The crew did seem to all be there, except for the person James would deem unnecessary. "If this might have to do with our new missions, shouldn't we call on Rhune? He should be here for this."

Maybe it was the long stories growing up that Vincent had listened to with rapt attention while sitting on Rhune's knee. Perhaps he couldn't throw the good of the man aside for the one mistake he made and his attempt to make amends that led to this. Or maybe a small part of him understood the need to have his soul mate at his side...regardless. But as gazes turned his way from all sides of the room, he shrugged. "Shouldn't he?"

The door opened, and the large man stepped into the hallowed room. He peered at the package in James' grip. "Yes, I believe I should." With a wave of his hand, the door closed behind him. "And as with all matters of the ethereal, the room should be sealed. *Eko silyst.*"

"And what do you know of this?" James' voice muffled, proof the silencing spell had taken effect. He lifted the bound booklet. "Was it you who put it in the basement for Mechenzie to find?"

Rhune's brows rose with his blink. He raked his fingers across his jaw and walked to the desk. "No."

"But?" James' tone left much to be disciplined. "You know what it is?"

"I'm afraid I don't, son."

James gnashed his teeth, obviously prepared to rebuttal with the whole, *I'm not your son,* denial. But Mianna interrupted the trade of words.

"I know what it is." She sounded like an angel in the wake of James' tension.

Everyone turned to look at her, and she stood from her seat beside Cole. "It's a book, and it has to do with me. However it got in the basement, it was meant for me to find. Rhune, Sylis, and Mechenzie are probably mentioned in it. Well, Mechenzie would be spoken of as Lilith, but I bet that's why it responded to her touch and glowed. She's Lilith."

Cole wrapped his arm around her waist and quietly spoke, though Vincent had no trouble overhearing the words. "Love, I know you're convinced of a book given to Father about you before you were born, but what would Rhune and Mechenzie have to do with it?"

Vincent scoffed. "Are you kidding me? A book was given to Father about Mianna before she was born?" A half-hearted chortle jiggled in his chest. "This only gets better and better."

Cole scowled and stretched to look at him around his shoulder. "Kid, this isn't a laughing matter."

"Let me guess." He sat straighter in his chair and allowed his light heart to show on his face. He didn't know where the punchiness was coming from but... Well, yes, he did know. His spirit had never felt so free, and he owed it all to his beautiful wife who happened to be at the back of the room disregarding all this stuffy talk.

Vincent lifted his hand as if to recite a poetic letter. "They're mentioned in this magic book because they're all part of this prophecy; including Mianna, who was chosen before she was born to fill a role in the whole thing. And I will take one guess what role that would be. Love. The whole time we've known Mianna, what was her one underlying virtue?"

"Love." Cole's scowl melted to allow his eyes to spark a look of curiosity.

Linda raised her hand as if she were in class and wanted a word. "That's right. Anna loved everyone and everything. It's why she couldn't be rude to Lord Dressen when he called on her."

James shook his head. "Mianna was her first life span. A soul isn't born with that kind of predestination. It grows and develops that quality as it learns."

"Exactly," said Cole.

Vincent nodded and looked at Rhune. "I think it's safe to say things are only going to get crazier as the secrets to the prophecy open to us. So," he turned his gaze to Mianna, but he could hardly see her profile beyond Cole. "What were you, really? A member of Arylin's court? Her personal handmaiden?"

Mianna placed her hand gently on Cole's arm and guided him aside so she could face Vincent full on. "I've been having...visions lately. Visions of things from my previous lives. And I swear by all that is good, I heard Arylin call to me

Charlene A. Wilson

numerous times. Like a sweet whisper. Not by any of my names of my lives, but...by a name that touches my very soul." Her voice hushed. "Iaami. And I don't know how, but I know that book is for me."

If anyone was shocked, they didn't say so, but the silence doubled as even the twins and Elaina turned their attention to her and listened.

"We all forget for a reason when we are born into mortality. How else could we develop the strength we will need to someday advance enough to become like those who created us?" She placed her palm on Cole's chest with a loving brush. "Even the oldest realm in the Spectrum, Meridian, holds souls who've advanced further than any, and yet are children, so far away from reaching the point of dwelling with the gods."

Cole gently placed his hand on hers and held it on the spot above his heart. Did she know her movement ceased there? Regardless, the old brood looked like anything but old...or a brood. His features had softened to the point he looked ten years younger, and Vincent didn't think he'd ever seen this brother so serene.

Vincent glanced at the others, held enrapt by Mianna's words. All seemed riveted, and he couldn't blame them. The air tasted sweeter and filled with a spirit that spoke to their souls. If he didn't know better, he'd swear Arylin, the Goddess of Love herself, would appear to bear witness of the truthfulness of the words.

A soft weep sounded, and he turned in time move aside as Elaina to rushed forth. But instead of facing him, she faced her sister-in-law. She rested her hand on Vincent's leg and then lowered herself to her knees.

"Oh, sweet Angel of Love," she whispered.

Vincent lifted his hand to place it on her back to...what? He didn't know. The Angel of Love, the one spoken of in the prophecy, stood the distance of Cole between them, and nobody corrected Elaina for kneeling before any other than her creators.

A soft glow emitted from Mianna's skin as she smiled the sweetest most charismatic smile her cherubic features could produce. A little laugh tickled the air. "Elaina, there's no need for that. I'm not a Goddess. Right now, I need the help of that book to remember the virtues I must learn from my lives that have been lost to me."

Chapter Fourteen

Bliss emanated from Anna's countenance, and Elaina subconsciously reached to touch the alluring skin. Her mind and body buzzed with veneration. She inhaled a shake breath and sugary air permeated her being. Her gut lurched at the sweetness, and she quickly swallowed to force the acid back where it belonged. It burned her esophagus.

In a haphazard attempt to flee, she threw her hand over her mouth and pushed against Vincent's knee to stand. "I'm sorry. I..."

Her stomach roiled, and she darted for the door. As she flung it open, the atmospheric pressure in the room diminished, and her rushed steps sounded three times as loud as they clattered on the hardwood floor.

Bathroom. I need a bathroom. She grabbed the lavatory handle at the end of the hall and threw the door wide. Slipping inside, she took a deep breath of the sarsaparilla-scented air to clear her senses.

Wrong thing to do!

Elaina dropped to her knees before the toilet as her stomach heaved. She didn't know she had eaten that much, or anything that would turn her body into an expel-the-snot-out-of-every-fiber machine.

Her arms quaked as she braced herself against the marble bowl. Shivers shook her breath, and she slid into a sitting position to control the tremors in her thighs.

"Elaina are you okay?" Vincent's voice sounded like a heavenly messenger despite the shock that laced his words.

Shame prickled her cheeks and rose to her ears. These people were so far beyond her. That beloved marvelous Meridian couldn't possibly be meant to be her match. A glorious man from an advanced civilization that conversed with the gods should never be subjected to a troll throwing up her guts. What was she thinking when she had prayed for his proposal? How could she let him see her like this?

"Oh, sweet mother of life, Vince." She turned to face the wall.

He knelt and braced her shoulders. "Communication with the ethereal can be overwhelming sometimes. I'll fly you to the room so you can lie down."

The thought of every fiber having the freedom to indeed expel snot sent a wave of panic through her. "Oh, no. No. I don't think I could handle being a million particles right now. I'd probably drip sick all the way up there."

"Okay." His arms wrapped around her waist and under her knees. "But you need to lie down."

"No, Vince, please. I want Linda."

"I'm here, little sister. Let me help you upstairs." Her sister appeared from behind Vincent and inched her way past him into the small room.

Elaina nodded. "Linda will help me. Just...go back to your meeting, Vince. I'll be all right. You can fill me in."

"Elaina."

The hurt in his voice tugged at her heart. The last thing she wanted to do was hurt him, but she couldn't face him. Face any of them.

Everyone in Shilo City and their cat seemed in attendance when Elaina emerged from the bathroom. She covered her face, as if that would hide the rest of her from the stunning Angel of Love and the four magnificent men of Meridian. How could she be accepted by these people when she was a lowly Terran?

As they ascended the stairs to their third-floor suite, Vincent quietly followed. Her chin quivered at the thought. I don't want him to watch me. He can't see me like this!

As they entered the room, he waved his hand, and the curtains slid, partially closing.

Elaina crawled into bed and rolled to her side to keep from looking into Vincent's eyes as he knelt beside her. Her voice only came out as a murmur "Thank you, Vince. Linda can help me now."

"Elaina there's nothing to be ashamed of. My first experience with a deity almost knocked me to the floor. You handled meeting an angel with grace."

"I threw up, Vince."

"The air was so much sweeter than you're used to. Don't let this get to you."

But she had. She couldn't help it. She'd acted like a child, stepped into an arena she had no business being in, and bowed to an angel, eliciting the being's emotions. Iaami had glowed!

"Vince, please leave. I need some time."

"Yeah. Okay."

His tone sounded as if she'd broken his heart, but right then, all Elaina wanted was to bury her face in her Terran sister's shoulder and cry; away from magical forces, away from ethereal beings.

As the door clicked, she sat up and reached for her big sister who'd protected her from bullies as they grew, who'd comforted her when her heart had been broken.

Linda's brows arched upward, and her head leaned in a sympathetic gesture. "Oh, little sister, don't be embarrassed." She sat beside Elaina and held her. "That sweetness about got to me. And I had to hold onto James' arm just to stay where I was and not do what you did."

A sob punched from Elaina's chest. "I can't face them."

"Shhh." Linda guided Elaina's head to rest on her bosoms and stroked her hair. "You don't have to. When you feel up to it, I'll call Vince in to help."

"I never want to see him again, Linda. What was I thinking? I'm not meant for all this."

"You were thinking you're in love. Face it, Elaina, you love a Meridian man. There's no shame in that, no matter how you look at it. They're amazing in their own right. Forget that they commune with gods and angels. These guys are hot, and they chose to have us in their lives. Just be yourself. It's what Vince fell in love with."

She made sense. Linda always did, it seemed; factual, forthright, Linda with her feet on the ground and fighting for what she thought was right.

A small squeak sounded in Elaina's throat as she tried to speak past the tightness. "I do love him. With all my soul. But Linda, I want to be special too. Vince deserves that. Nothing about me is any different than any of his other wives he's had on Terra."

Linda huffed. "You're kidding me, right? Hasn't he told you that you're his soul mate? The way I understand it that's the highest form of love there is for them. He'll search for you from now to eternity." She shook her head. "James hasn't told me that. Nothing near it. But I'm not sobbing into your boobs, am I?"

Laughter popped from Elaina's lungs. "No." She sat up and swiped the tears from her cheeks. "But you gave James something no one has ever given any of them."

"Like what?"

"A chance to be a father."

Chapter Fifteen

Mianna released the tie on the package, and Cole hardly held back his anticipation. He tapped his fingers to his thumb and watched the thin twine fall away from the parchment. What would his love have to do with his father, and why would a book be given to him that had to do with her lives? No wonder the man found interest in the woman who'd fallen in love with his son. But to the point of wanting her for himself? Were they meant to be together all along? Did Mianna fall in love with the wrong Shilo?

He scratched his palms with his fingernails to dispel the itch. Surely, she hadn't felt the same attraction to Sylis as she had to him. She had, after all, refused his attentions over several life spans.

James held up his hand. "Shouldn't we wait for Linda and Elaina to return? This will affect them if it affects us."

A knock came at the study door, and as if she'd heard his concern, Linda entered with a nodded. "I have a feeling this must do with all of us. I want to be here."

Vincent stood. "Where's Elaina?"

"She's lying down.

"Should I go to her?"

Linda squelched her cheek. "I think she really wants to be totally alone, Vince. Sorry."

Patience wavering, Cole shuffled his feet. "Let's just get this underway. You can fill her in later, Kid."

At Vincent's nod, Rhune sealed the study. "*Eko silyst.*"

The room entombed them in protective silence.

Mianna gently pealed the parchment way from the book, and a soft glow enveloped the tome in an ellipse. She sucked in a deep breath as the cover opened at her gentle touch. Chromatic swirls filled the pages and, as if by instinct, Mianna placed her hands on them. Bright beams of multicolored light shot through the spaces between her fingers and thumbs. Her eyes opened wide as a cloud of mist bathed her face.

"They are virtues." The awe in her voice came forth breathy. "I was to learn these during my lives on Terra."

Her pupils grew within the light, and Cole's cheek twitched as he wanted to squint for her. Though he knew she opened her soul to handle as much as she could, Mianna couldn't be prepared for this. Morals often endured discomfort to

communicate with or see ethereal planes—
their duties as Sentinels required it many
times—but to have your pupils widen when
nature would contract them to protect from
harm...

Her lower lip quivered, nostrils flared,
and her brows rose to mid-way up her
forehead. Goosebumps appeared on her
arms, and her hands flinched on the book.

"Mianna?"

"There are so many." She slowly shook
her head. "And I'm to understand the
feelings and consequences of them all.
Oh...I chose to come here to help one man
remember who he is, and what his true goal
must be. This book, the book of the
experiences I needed to learn here on
Cornerstone Deep, contains things I must
try to recall and put into perspective before
I meet him again... or I could fail."

Cole placed his hand on her back for
support. "We're all here to help you, my
love."

A small nod relayed she'd heard him,
but her attention didn't vary from the book.
"Unconditional love. It's the one underlying
goal of every circumstance... And what I
must remind Allant when the time comes
for his decision."

Ambrosia swirls filtered from the
chromatic pages, and a loving voice spoke,

familiar, gentle.

"Iaami," it sang, as if calling her home. "It is time."

Veneration flowed from every soul, joining with Cole's. Mandy and Mechenzie came into his periphery, quiet awe on their little faces.

White light settled around Mianna, and the scent of roses touched Cole's senses. As if the study melted away, a vision of the beautiful pink and white flowers surrounded the gathered family members. Mianna closed her eyes and breathed deeply, no doubt savoring the fresh scent. As if she could touch the flora, she slowly brushed her hands through the air. "Hmm. I've longed to roam these fields. It has been so long."

Arylin's loving voice rode a slight breeze within the vision. "You've been gone for a time among the mortals. Have you learned what you hoped to find?"

Riveted, Cole watched Mianna's smile fade.

She gazed toward the misted horizon. "I'm afraid I've lost much. As Mianna I have learned of the love I will need. As Anna...I find her strength carried her through some most difficult times."

"Yes. But the lifetimes you have lost through the transformation would have also aided you in your task."

Cole lowered his gaze. He didn't need to be reminded of his failure. It seemed at every turn, the consequences mounted. But this moment was for Mianna. For her learning and counsel with her Goddess. Perhaps it was mercy that allowed the rest of them to experience the moment that they may help Mianna in her mission. He leaned his head to the side as he witnessed the divine conversation.

A ladybug fluttered onto Mianna's finger, and her soft smile returned as Arylin spoke.

"If you wish to abandon the promise, you may do so, my sweet sister. No one will expect you to fulfill a task when the gift, through no fault of your own, was maimed."

All gazes turned to view Mianna.

Sister? She's the Goddess of Love's sister? What was Cole thinking? It could only be the truth. Her entire life as Mianna had been proof of her deepest nature. No other looked beyond outward appearance to the goodness within without judgment. No other accepted a person for who they were to the extent Mianna had.

Lifting her hand high, Mianna helped the ladybug launch into flight. "What other important things must I know that I had learned but lost, Arylin?"

The ambrosia swirls floated to clothe the glorious Goddess of Love as she appeared. Her golden hair rested on the downy feathers at her shoulders and then flowed the length of her back in thick waves.

Silence held the room as Arylin's sky blue eyes peered at only Mianna. Cole had to wonder if Linda and the girls could see the Goddess. He knew the rest of them did.

Linda's hands rested on her bosoms as she sank to her knees. Mandy and Mechenzie's wide gazes didn't vary from where Arylin stood. Yes, they could see the ethereal being.

"Iaami, my darling little sister. I knew you would not back away." She took Mianna's hands in a gentle hold. "I will help every way I can, but it is your heart and soul that must learn from these things. Study the book Father and Mother have prepared for you. Use insight to relate all teachings to the experiences I will show you. Contemplate and study reactions, and most of all, relate love to each outcome."

"I will. And with the help of everyone here, I know I will succeed."

Reverence flushed Cole's heart, and his soul wanted to weep out of love for her.

Arylin nodded, but her gaze didn't leave her little sister. Soft wisps of burgundy and sage surrounded her as she squeezed Iaami's hands and then let go. She faded along with the light showing around Mianna.

It seemed no one dared speak for fear of disturbing the glorious moment.

Vincent's whisper could barely be heard within the silencing spell of the room. "You really are the Angel of Love."

Mianna slowly stroked the page of the book. As the ellipse faded, she spoke as if she hadn't heard him. "I know I have help from heaven and from all of you. But to relay the message to Allant in a way that he will know I understand; that I'd experienced the needs he had..." She looked at Cole, a sadness in her beautiful blue eyes. "Cole, how can I experience so much in such a short time?"

Regret hit him anew. He'd done this. He'd taken the precious moments that had taught her how to complete her call by casting that blasted spell and sealing it with his kiss. Arylin's words from the night of her transformation flashed in his memory.

"Advancement made over her last five life cycles has been lost. A crippling toll for a soul to pay."

Very crippling, considering this new information. A deep flush burned his cheeks. Would the consequences of that one unharnessed kiss ever be completed? The tragic unbinding attempt on her soul, the loss of five life times, and then glorious reprieve as Gryffin, the God of Conformance, pronounced judgment for him to serve Mianna for the rest of his existence.

But it was all for not, as he was to fulfill a mission on a faraway dimension, away from the love he swore to protect.

He expelled the hot breath that filled his lungs as further realization of the situation hit him. Mianna was the Angel of Love from the prophecy, chosen to sway his father into making the right choice that would save a world and his soul. And that meant she would be accompanying him to Midway Summit.

A puff of laughter shot from his lips. Inappropriate at the moment, but he couldn't help it. This couldn't be more perfect!

How did the counsel know? What am I thinking? The Gods instruct the counsel who only performed their duty and relayed their wishes.

Renewed honor to the gods filled Cole, and he pulled Mianna into an embrace. His arms tightened around her, holding her close to his heart. "The Gods will guide you, my love. You'll accomplish this mission with favor."

Vincent's thoughts broke into Cole's mind with clarity. *"Sorry to break into all this, but will I accomplish my assignment with favor? James expects me to fill Mother's role. Cole. I don't' know faintest of these things."*

The unspoken question caused Cole to wonder. How soon would the prophecy take place? Vincent could never manage the knowledge of an aged soul, in wisdom or skill, in such a short time. Cole had once said he believed Vincent was born to fulfill a purpose, other than to fill the third member of the Triad in the family. Could this be it? But a soul is the greatest source of strength and stability a being can have.

He looked at the little girl, standing beside her sister. Mechenzie had such a soul and the answer came strong to his mind.

She would need to be trained to fill the role of her previous life as Lilith.

Cole looked at James, standing at the head station of the desk, jawline clenched, and lips pressed tightly together.

"James, you know, don't you," he said, sending his thoughts to James through his gift. *"You know how this must be done. She could train in Meridian. She would learn*

quickly, and the time would seem short to Cornerstone Deep standards."

James' response came in the form of a telepathic statement. *"I can't take her to Meridian without Linda and Mandy, Cole. It would break her mother's heart."*

Cole cleared his throat. "For this mission to succeed, we'll need the strongest most pure talent available in Mother's position."

Vincent looked to the side, and then lowered his gaze to the carpet. "And that's not me."

Rhune placed his hands at his waist.

James' low tone revealed his hesitancy to agree. "We can't separate the family

Linda's brows jumped. "What family?"

Rhune held out his hand in Mandy's direction. "That little girl and the mother won't have any place in Meridian. They're Terran. Even with my blessing, the stay would shorten their lives considerably."

"Wait. Are you talking about Kenzie? You're not taking my baby." Linda rushed around the desk and positioned herself between the men and her girls. "Taravaughn said she could stay. That she could stay if..." Color drained from the woman's face as she quietly finished the sentence. "Your gods find favor."

Rhune nodded. "And clearly, she's

needed elsewhere."

His tone couldn't have been blunter, and Cole growled before James had a chance.

"No!" Linda's screech filled the enchanted room and wrenched Cole's heart.

James dashed from the desk and wrapped her in his arms. "Now, Leenja, please."

"She's my baby! Mine! She was given to me to protect and love. I won't let you take her to some other worldly dimension I know nothing about. I can't!" She spun out of James' hold, lowered into a squat, and threw her hands wide.

The little girls rushed into her arms.

Thoughts whirled from Linda's mind and rammed into Cole's consciousness.

I'll run with them, hide! In the deepest places on Terra, we'll hide.

Pity weighed Cole's gaze downward. *Oh Linda. Don't you know; you can't hide from the gods?*

Shilo Manor series~Destiny

Chapter Sixteen

Elaina rolled onto her back and looked at the newly refurbished chandelier above her. Vincent had done a beautiful job of reassembling it. Even though it took three tries to get it all right. Thank heavens he didn't call on James like he'd wanted.

She dragged her hands down her face, pity eating at her heart. "I'm being such a baby, but I don't belong around these people. I have nothing to offer them."

Squirrels chattered outside the west side window, and Elaina rolled her head on the pillow to see the cheery things. Muted light filtered through the tree limbs and leaves while the lively little souls scampered among them. She furrowed her brows as she focused beyond, to the darkening sky. *The sun is going down? How did it get so late so fast?*

She didn't think she had fallen asleep. Her mind whirled. Vince did say time fled when the ethereal was present. And Anna has definitely become an ethereal being. "Her skin glowed like liquid gold," she said to the squirrels, as if they'd hear her. "And when she laughed it was like a tinkle on the breeze. *Iaami.* How beautiful is that?"

Throwing her hands to her face, she attempted to make it all disappear: the images of Iaami, the vomit session, and her close relationship with Sentinels of Cornerstone Deep. "What am I doing here? Gods, I don't belong!"

Tears welled under her lids again, and she pressed her palms to her eyes. Was that why Venus hadn't answered her prayers? No, she couldn't believe that. The Goddess loved to be prayed to and answer humble prayers. Doubt whispered another possible answer. *She's a Goddess of Midway Summit, not Terra.*

Light spilled over the foot of the bed as Vincent opened the door and quietly stepped inside. He closed it behind him.

She barely heard him whisper something over the jabber of birds. Gnawing the inside of her cheek, she slowly let her hand slide to the side of her face and feigned sleep.

The light from the bathroom illuminated the room as he turned it on. A moment later, water ran, and clothes rustled.

He's getting ready for bed already?

The mattress dipped as he sat down, and the weight of his hand sat on her hip. "Elaina?"

How could she face him? How could she ever look into those beautiful ebony eyes again without feeling like the puny soul she was? She moaned with a little stretch as she rolled to her side.

The comforter tugged across the bed as he joined her, and then his arm rested around her waist.

A cringe tightened her lips. It burned, his gentle touch; the touch of greatness. If only Venus would answer her pleas for a child. It would prove she was worthy of a Meridian man's love. She could hold her head high and stand at Vincent's side, proud, knowing with a certainty that her destiny was anchored.

She peered out the window across the room from her, and then beyond. The granite bluff stood proud past the woodlands and held the portal to the other realms.

Could a god from another dimension hear prayers when spoken here? Perhaps the reason the goddess hadn't granted her desire was because it hadn't reached her. If she were closer to the doorway to Venus's throne, her prayers would be heard, surely. Her wish was a righteous one, after all. How could a deity who loved to bless mortals with that gift deny the request if she heard it?

Sucking her lower lip between her teeth, Elaina set her plan. *As soon as he's asleep, I think I'll take a stroll.*

~ * ~

A multitude of crickets seemed to have migrated to the backyard along with the loudest peacocks Elaina had ever heard. She trotted across the terrace and halted with a jolt as Anna walked from the topiary entrance. *Gods, I didn't expect anyone to be out here. Especially her!*

She took a deep breath and strolled across the lush lawn to meet her, hoping her weak knees wouldn't buckle. "Hi Anna. I'm just going for a walk. Kinda want to think, you know? Nothing special. Just to think. The topiary is beautiful, isn't it?"

She ended her jabber with a tweak of her lips. Could an Angel of Love read through her lie? Lying had never been a talent of hers to begin with.

"Oh yes, the topiary is one of my favorite places when I have things cluttering my mind. The serenity helps me iron things out a bit." She smiled.

"Right. That's what I want to do. Iron some things out in my head." She motioned toward the pathway through the blooms. "So... I'll just...go."

"Okay, Elaina. Have a good night." Anna hesitated as she met Elaina's gaze, but then headed for the back door to Shilo Manor.

Air rushed from Elaina's pursed lips, and she rolled her eyes. *Thank the Gods I didn't drop and show praise to Iaami on the spot.* "Okay, I am going for a walk. Just not in there."

Her feet crunched the twigs on the forest bed, and her legs twitched with each snap. The world teemed with life. Frogs sang while night birds accompanied them overhead. Owls hooted, a community of squirrels scampered across her path and then up the trees, and a myriad of insects seemed to choose that night to be noticed. If Rhune hadn't told her of the area's safe enchantment, she'd be shivering from fright instead of the chill.

The light from her lamp reflected off the tall trunks, making them look as if they were painted onto shadow. White petals floated from the overhead branches to her path as she walked. The aroma of apricot blossoms mixed with the dusty scent of dried leaves and the earthy smell oddly comforted her. She walked, veering from her path only to avoid snares and fallen tree limbs.

As she broke through the edge of the arbors, dusk had gone to bed for the night, and the moon shown its bright mid-ascent to the heavens. Beams from the great orb highlighted the landing and made it look like an alien obstacle course created by the Shilos during their fight with Lord Dressen. It seemed a mile long, as she couldn't make out the large boulder that had landed beside the portal during Vincent's battle to protect the gateway to the planes.

The scene returned to her mind, stunning and vivid: Her love's noble stance, his bold face looking directly at the Grand Marshal as a ribbon of brilliant power arched over his head plied by his fists. Every charge of magic Lord Dressen had fired, Vincent met with a fierce lunge. The collision of magic had shaken the atmosphere, and when James caused the boulder that fell from above to veer from its path, the world rocked as it struck the ground. Wild charges had shot from Lord Dressen's hands as he turned in the center of a whirlwind of rubble that scarred the earth.

A breeze blew from Oberon Sea, and Elaina filled her lungs with the salty air. Recalling the location of the portal, she set her course. *Just put one foot in front of the other. I have to make it at some point if I head straight to the mountainside.*

She pressed her fist into her palm and flexed her biceps to relieve the nervous excitement. Would Venus speak to her? Show herself? Even a finger would be such a welcomed sight. Elaina could imagine herself fainting on the spot. But one thing she knew in her heart; her prayer would be granted. It had to be.

As she neared, the beam from her flashlight touched a boulder twice her height and just as wide that looked like part of the mountain from a distance. Her heart skipped.

Rushing to the right, she scanned the foot of the bluff for anything that resembled the arched doorway she had seen Vincent protect. Scuffs and gouges from Lord Dressen's charges littered the rock face, but nothing else proved the portal existed.

"This isn't right. It was here." She ran her fingertips along the layers of sediment. "How am I going to get to Midway Summit if I can't even find the portal?"

As she spoke the words, "Midway Summit," neon beams poured through tiny cracks in the rock. She backed away with a gasp as the cracks widened, and the rock fell away, creating a tall arch. Light seeped inward, filling the outlined space with a multitude of colors.

Air puffed from Elaina's lips, and then her lungs refused to take another breath. Squinting to relieve the sting of brightness, she lifted her arm to shield her eyes from the rays.

White light overtook the gateway to the realms as she took a step back and then lowered her hand to her side. Her chest ached as she sucked in the sugary scent of the light. "Sweet Venus, it's beautiful!" *And I promise not to throw up. I promise to…*

As her mind whirled with ways to plea to the loving deity, her heart longed to be as near as possible. *If she hears me at the portal, how much greater would it be in her realm? It would show that my whole soul desires her help. I can always come back after I've prayed, after I've worshipped the goddess I've chosen to be my patron god.*

Lost in veneration, her hands raised in praise, her feet moved forward, and Elaina stepped into a white void.

Charlene A. Wilson

Chapter Seventeen

All eyes turned toward the entrance as Cole entered Dressen's memorial service, flanked by James and Vincent. The ballroom peaked at the center, support beams meeting at a high arch like a cathedral, and then sloped to host the second and third level balconies. The last time they'd been in this room, Cole had deliver the gift that led to all this; the memory pearl. How could he have known the Grand Marshal shared the same soul his father had? How could he have known it would aid in partially fulfilling a prophecy?

A hush fell over the crowd, and a myriad of telepathic opinions hit him. He attempted to shove them aside. The last thing he needed was to know everyone's thoughts on what had happened that day in Shilo Park. Obviously, the good people now knew for certain the Founders were more than just those who established their capitol city. They were connected with the gods, and in turn must be reverenced...or at least shown respect beyond the crude nickname of the Wizards of Shilo Manor.

Cole suppressed a snarl at the thought. *The Wizards of Shilo Manor.*

The fact Cole had a hand in Dressen's death didn't seem to faze those in attendance as he couldn't block out all the mental images going through their minds. Heart attack, the grand fight, magical spells—everyone seemed to have their own ideas of what had happened.

But, none blamed him? Cole cleared his throat. None but the Gods...and himself.

Vincent leaned close, his lips quirked. "Really. Neither of you have seen Elaina? This isn't like her."

James shook his head. "I thought you were going to check with Linda."

"She hadn't seen her either."

Cole's response rumbled in his throat as he didn't want to speak too loudly. "Mianna was up early. Elaina probably went to the topiary with her. Now let's get this appearance taken care off so we can get back."

Dressen's twin sister appeared in his periphery, and Cole straightened with a smile. For as deplorable the Grand Marshal had been, his sister was just as kind; charity balls, worship to the Gods, soup kitchens for the homeless, all note-worthy contributions.

"Sir Cole, please come in and join the celebration of Kyle's life."

"Lady Kendra. I'm honored to have been invited to such a celebration." He gingerly lifted Kendra's extended hand and kissed the top of her palm.

"The honor is ours that you have accepted. As it is to have Sir Vincent and Sir James." She bowed her head to the two as she spoke their names. Her brows rose. "But your sweet Ladies have not joined you?"

"Our apologies. Under the circumstances, Anna felt she must decline. And as Anna's closest friends, Elaina and Linda felt they must support her."

"Oh, everybody knows how Kyle manipulated that poor girl. I'm just pleased the whole situation ended happily for her."

She motioned toward the left of the great hall. The exclamatory bar sat nestled within the corner, surrounded by lush lounges and soft lighting. "Do enjoy some of Brother's fine liqueur. He stocked the best, as I've been told."

A soft chortle sounded in her throat as she turned and took a few steps away. Cole followed while James and Vincent took the hint and veered toward the bar.

"I know it's a little off beat to hold a service such as this in the home of the departed, but I simply didn't have the room in mine. I'm still at a loss as to what I'll do with all his belongings. Being his only living relative, he left it to me."

Kendra lifted her drink and turned in a small circle. "I mean, look at this place. I told him on several occasions that there was enough room in this hall alone to house every homeless person in the city. And they'd even have a mini topiary to roam, over there in the corner, when they wanted a stroll. Did you know there's a cathedral on the second floor for worship to Arylin? I never knew him to be the praying kind, but there you have it."

"We mustn't judge Lord Dressen by the way he acquired Anna. He treated his servants well. They loved him, in his way, I'm sure. Perhaps he had it built for them. And perhaps it would be an excellent idea to continue his exemplary service, Lady Kendra."

"What do you mean?"

"Why not turn Lord Dressen's Mansion into managed housing for the less fortunate? Instead of allowing the people to remember him for his last act of selfishness upon an innocent young woman, let his memory be of service and compassion to the homeless."

"Why, Sir Cole. That is the most gracious thing I've ever heard. He did, after all, try to kill you to have the girl."

Maybe it was a last attempt at salvaging the soul of his father's memory, but Cole couldn't help himself. As much as he hated Lord Dressen and his gaudy taste in flaunting his wealth, patching the man's reputation could only help these people cope with what had happened to the man they'd admired.

"I'm merely suggesting a positive outcome for all that has happened."

"And a beautiful idea. That's exactly what shall be done." She lifted her glass to him and then drank.

Cole reached into his pocket and removed a brass box. "Lady Kendra, I'm aware of the distance between you and Lord Dressen over the past years. Bitter memories should have no place in our lives when a loved one departs. I've prepared a special gift for you."

Kendra placed her hand on her breasts. "For me? Why Sir Cole, I never expected any form of gratuity here. I've done nothing. Lord Carrington and Kyle's servants arranged everything. I merely showed up."

Cole shook his head. "This is for you alone, for the comfort of your soul." He motioned for her to open her hand, and then tilted the lid of the box open. "This gift I give will allow you to call upon any memory you have of you and your brother at any time in your life. I understand you are twins. Twins have a special connection, a bond like no other sibling. They are rare, and few know of this. I wish you to have this gift for when you are lonely and seek comfort."

A tear crested Kendra's lashes as she breathed an *O*. She opened her hand, and Cole pinched at the pale blue cloud within the box. It followed his motion as he led it to settle in her palm. Azure swirled into a little pearl, lighter hues encircling it like clouds from the heavens. With the gem solidified, Cole closed her hand to embrace it with his fingers.

"Keep it close. Any memory of the two of you in this life will come to your mind as if you are reliving them. Let this be a special gift. From the one who caused your brother's death."

Her airy response portrayed her astonishment, though Cole sensed insecurity as she gazed at her closed hand. "Oh my. Such an extraordinary gift."

"Please know this gift is unlike the one I gave to your brother. His memory pearl could call on any memory in his life. And he chose to use it unwisely. This is a simple memory album specialized to call upon moments the two of you shared."

A smile lit her face and genuine thanks poured from her emotions. "Then I graciously accept with a whole heart, Sir Cole. Thank you."

"My pleasure."

James' voice came to his mind, and the grave tone sent a chill up his neck. *"Cole. We need to talk."*

Cole glanced to his left and found his brothers looking at him, Vincent with a scowl and James pale. "My apologies, Lady Kendra, but I see that I'm needed elsewhere."

"Oh, I do hope that means elsewhere here at the celebration."

James and Vincent grasped the edge of their cloaks, and Cole shook his head. "I'm afraid not. But my deepest wishes for your family's happiness."

"And yours, Sir Cole."

Cole bowed his head and then stepped back. Turning for the door, he set a long-paced stride. His brothers followed suit and together their piqued strides hammered the floor above the din of conversation. Guests backed away, giving the three wide berth as they left the hall. As soon as they crossed the mansion ingress, Cole grasped the edge of his cloak and flung the panel high. On cue, James and Vincent dispersed into the Smoke of Night with him, and they flew into the bright morning sky.

Crisp spring air permeated Cole's elements as they darted over the neighborhood of elite homes toward the manor. He sent his thoughts to James. *"So, what's this about?"*

"Lord Carrington, Dressen's right-hand man. He knows where the portal is; saw Vince defending it from Dressen when he drove Elaina and Linda to the landing in search of him. And he's been talking. So much so that other noblemen are taking notice. There's rumor of a planned breach."

Chapter Eighteen

A deep sigh issued from Rhune's lips as he placed the family Candle Vignette on the desk in front of him. He willed the first image to appear as he waved his hand at the fissure in the top of the cylinder. A picture of his brother undulated in the flame as it flickered to life.

"How young and confident you were, Sylisan. How sure you were of your destiny among the realms."

He passed his finger over the flame as if turning the page of a book, and a perfect family shown bright against the rays of the portal to the realms. "The day they arrived, no doubt."

With each new picture, Rhune's heart sank further. The innocence in Vincentor's eyes, the life in Colhart's smile, and the pride on Jamesuranton's face as he looked upon the man who posed as his father all seemed a lifetime ago. Yet, it was so close he could hear the joyful banter between the three, feel the pressure his brother's embrace, and the tantalizing touch of Lilith; his love and soul mate. What a cruel twist, to find an eternal companion in your brother's wife.

"If only I'd found you first, my sweet dove. How things would have been different."

A little voice carried through the foyer and down the hall to the study, and Rhune waved at the Vignette to dim the images.

"But Momma, I like it here. Poppa James plays with us. And Uncle Vincent and Aunt Elaina are here."

"I know, Mandy pop," answered her mother. "But we need to go on a fast trip. We'll get to see your father. Don't you want to see him for a while?"

"I...guess."

Another young tone joined them. "Here, you can take Clifford the Clown Mandy. He's always there. And I promise I won't let anything happen to you. Really, I promise."

There was a pause.

"Okay, girls less chatter and more walking. The cabbie is meeting us half a mile up the hill." Feet shuffled, and Linda's voice trembled as she spoke quietly. "Let's play a game. The first one to the taxi gets a chocolate fudge sundae."

"A chocolate fudge Sunday?" A little girl squealed. "No fair if Kenzie turns into a ghost to get there quicker!"

"This isn't a trip. This is about taking me to training. Isn't it?"

Rhune groaned. "Ah, Linda." Lifting his hand toward the Utopian, he summoned the mirror-crowned instrument. It lighted on the desk before him. The three circular mirrors clicked into place, and a hologram of the voluptuous blonde and two blondettes formed above the tulip stage.

Mechenzie's grown up words and tone set pride in Rhune's heart. "It's my destiny, Momma. How can I run away from my destiny?"

Linda knelt before her daughter and pulled her close. "Mechenzie May. There is no such thing as a destiny that can't be changed. We make our own destiny by the decisions we make and the things we do. And right now, I'm making it my destiny to protect you." She took the girls' hands in hers. "You and Mandy Kay, you're the most precious things in my life and all that matter to me right now."

Tears brimmed her eyes as she pulled them into a hug. "Now, let's take a walk to meet the cab. Then, we can stop for ice cream before a nice long drive."

"But I don't want to go, Momma."

"And neither do I."

Linda's hushed voice carried almost as much as the children's had. "We don't have a choice, girls. We're going."

Rhune leaned back into his chair and watched the hologram of the trio as they exited the manor, trotted across the lawns, down the street, and then climbed into a waiting transport.

He chuckled to himself. "My dear Terran Tiger Lily."

Chapter Nineteen

Apricot leaves swirled on the front porch of Shilo Manor and then into the foyer as the door flung wide. Cole led the way over the threshold, toward the study, and barely caught sight of Mianna as she met them at a run.

How did she know we would be home early?

She followed as they darted down the hall and through the laurel-framed door.

As they formed beyond the ingress, Mianna slipped inside, and Vincent closed the door.

Rhune propped his feet on the cherry-wood desk and opened his mouth, poised to speak when Cole held up his hand and headed for the Master station. "*Eko silyst.*"

Catching his error mid-stride, he stepped to the side to allow James his rightful place as Head of Sentinels. "Apologies," he murmured and cocked the unoccupied counselor's chair to the side.

James grinned and took his seat. "No need."

With a grunt, Rhune kicked his heels to the floor and leaned his elbows on his knees. "We have a little situation that came to light while you boys were away."

Mianna nodded, over exuberance in her agreement. "I've discovered something too."

James rested into the back cushion of his chair. "It seems we all have urgent information."

A scoff came from beside the door, and Vincent folded his arms with his signature lean on the jam. "Why is it things all seem to happen at once around here?"

"Well, I wouldn't worry too much at this point over my news," said Rhune.

Shoving aside his curiosity, Cole looked at James. "But I believe your information may be more time sensitive. What's this about the noblemen wanting to breach the portal?"

A chorus of baritone and soprano sounded as Rhune and Mianna questioned at the same time. "What?"

James nodded. "Lord Standish informed me as soon as we got to the event. He's very concerned, and as he's one of the most faithful in the courts, I'm inclined to believe him. If anything intends to harm the righteous, he'll stand against it. He and Dressen clashed on many occasions. Right now, it's mostly talk. Though some want to act fast to throw us off. The majority say not to attempt a breach until they have a plan in place."

"That's right." Vincent chuckled. "News of me fighting off Dressen is a highly-noted conversation. Not many want to face a ribbon of power without big backup."

"Or a whirlwind of rubble," added James. "Cole, I'm calling for you to prepare a seal for the door to the realms. I won't have a situation that will call for the need of a life's essence to complete the task."

Cole's gaze dropped as he recalled the image of his father doing just that. The nightmares haunted him still. He sat in his chair, stretched one leg forward, and bent the other as he leaned back. "I'll get started on that."

With a nod, James looked at Vincent. "I'll call on you to stay in close touch with Lord Standish. He'll keep us informed."

"Will do."

Mianna's fingers tapped her thighs, and her gaze jumped among them as they spoke. "I really think I should tell you my news next."

Rhune waved his hand through the air. "By all means, my Terran angel. Mine can wait. They won't get so far as to not be tracked."

This time, all voices joined in the chord. "What?"

"Oh, James' lovely Tiger Lily took the

little ones and grabbed a transport, bags in hand. I can only assume she is trying to run from the inevitable." He motioned toward the Utopian. "I can pull them up when you're ready. I have them on scry."

James dragged his hand down his face and heaved a sigh. "Leenja."

"But, as I have said, it can wait. What is your urgent news, sweet angel?"

Mianna's fingers grasped each other. "I've noticed since I experienced the book that I'm more sensitive. Like I can understand so much more. It might be to help me learn how people feel going through things, so I don't have to experience them first hand, I'm not sure. But I ran into Elaina last night, before she went for a walk in the topiary to clear her mind."

She walked the length of the study and then turned. "I didn't realize it at the time, but I felt so many strong feelings of reverence and...determination coming from her. And it was in connection with the Goddess Venus from Midway Summit."

Vincent's arms dropped to his sides. "I knew something was up."

Mianna nodded. "I'm afraid...I'm afraid she went in search of Venus to pray."

James leaned his head. "Well, it's not right to pray to gods other than your own, but we can't stop her from doing it."

Vincent shook his head. "But all night?"

"The topiary is safe. No strangers or animals will harm her with the charm on the grounds."

"You don't understand, James." Vincent lifted from his lean. "Elaina doesn't like to be alone for long, especially at night."

Mianna's fingers knotted. "And I got the distinct feeling the topiary wasn't her final destination."

~ * ~

The void seemed to swallow Elaina as if she had been stuffed into a large white balloon. She lifted her hand to feel the enclosure, and then extended her arm. Nothing. Nothing but bright white. With an apprehensive hitch in her throat, she glanced down to see the platform she stood on. Dizziness whirled her mind as the emptiness extended beneath her feet.

Flailing her arms, she attempted to catch herself from falling into nothingness. A muffled scream ended at her lips, and she stumbled over what wasn't there. Ripples of light shadows puddled around her and quickly dispersed.

Closing her eyes, she sucked in air to cleanse her lungs. Calm replaced panic with the breath. Slowly lifting her lids, she focused straight ahead. *Okay, Elaina. You can do this. It's a portal to take you where you want to go. So...go.*

Her foot trembled as she stepped along the walkway that wasn't there and felt as if the floor moved with her instead of past her. Her motion warped like apparitions and reminded her of heat waves coming off a hot engine in the wintertime. *One, two, three steps. Okay, you did good. Now let's make sure you're really moving.*

Balancing on the balls of her feet, she turned at one-hundred-eighty degrees and walked three steps the way she came.

Then four.

And then five.

Heat rushed to her cheeks, and she quickly strode several more. *Where's the doorway? I know I turned completely to face behind me.* She knotted her fingers in her blouse, mimicking the knots in her stomach. *Oh, sweet Venus, what did I do?*

Elaina spun in every direction, looking for something, anything to anchor herself. Not a speck of dirt floated before her eyes. A hiccup forced its way past her tight throat. Tears brimmed the corners of her lids.

She broke into a run. "Oh, somebody, please help me!"

Her voice warbled as if she'd screamed under water. She jarred to a stop and ripples rode the motion behind her feet as if she skidded on an invisible trail within the void.

"Venus, my Goddess, hear me!" Her voice came forth in spasms as she directed her call to the scrying watch on her wrist. She gulped as if to swallow the non-existent liquid. "I'm in the portal! I think I'm lost. Please, please hear me." A squeak ended her plea as a sharp pain thickened her lower abdomen. Grasping her stomach, she sobbed and fell to her knees.

Why hadn't she listened to Anna? Hadn't she told her of the settlers from Cornerstone Summit? They barely made it to Midway, and that was with the help of Sylis Shilo, the renowned realm traveler.

Her whisper passed her lips as a prayer. "Oh, I don't want to die. Great Goddess Venus, please help me get to Midway Summit."

Chapter Twenty

Vincent folded his arms across his chest, and then glared at his uncle. The results didn't make sense, no matter how he looked at it.

Rhune shook his head as he cut a side glance at the empty Utopian mirrors. "I'm telling you, my boy, the Utopian isn't picking up on your Terran butterfly. Anywhere."

At times like these, Vincent could do without the charming pet names. "But how can that be? Have you tried the surrounding townships? If she's not staying at her parents' home, maybe she took a bus somewhere."

"I performed an advanced scry to take in all of Cornerstone Deep." His voice softened. "She doesn't show."

"She'd have to be dead to not show. And Elaina is not dead." Vince raked his fingers through his hair. "I'd know it."

Cole's low tone edged Vincent's nerves and caused the hair on his arms to prickle. "Run an essence trace. If something did happen to her, it'd show a date of death."

Mianna covered her mouth with her fingertips.

Vincent stepped into a turn and then jolted to a stop. "She's not *dead*!"

At Cole's words, Rhune spoke slowly to the Utopian. "Essence trace, Elaina Cantrell Shilo."

Words hit Vincent's mind, and he listened closely as they flashed in his understanding. As many times as he'd wished the creator of the instrument had placed a slower tempo to an answered trace, he wanted it to get to the point as soon as possible then.

"Crystal Everett McCallister, born Cornerstone Deep, Terra, 1876-1953. Elaina Cantrell Shilo, 1953-untraceable."

Aside from Vincent being startled that Elaina had lived a previous life—and been married—greater frustration exploded. He tossed his hand toward the Utopian and rouge sparks pocked the cherry-wood desk. "Untraceable? What's *that* supposed to mean?"

James blinked with his sigh and waved his hand. The pocks disappeared beneath a new finish.

Cole leaned his elbow on his knee. "Cool it, Kid. It means she's still alive. Just not within the search's reach."

"Which means..." James' gaze turned to the bookshelf the same time Cole's and

Rhune's did. The Triad globes glowed softly on the center shelf.

Was this yet another thing his father and brothers neglected to tell him as they performed their Sentinel duties? "Wait. Now what does it mean when they glow like that?"

Rhune sighed. "Well, it doesn't mean they're warm and happy sitting there together."

For once, Cole and Vincent seemed to share James' irritation with their uncle. They all scowled at him.

"It seems a breach has already taken place," said James.

Vincent clenched his fingers into fists and a familiar charge heated his knuckles. "She brought up how easy it was to travel the portal after Uncle Rhune told his stories. But I never expected her to *try* it."

Cole turned to Vincent. "Haven't you discussed the *dangers* of the portal with your woman?"

He glared at Cole as the comment wedged anger in his gut. "Her name is Elaina!"

Mianna stepped forward as if he'd said nothing. "I told her and Linda of those from Cornerstone Summit. That they almost died in their attempt to travel the spectrum."

"Yet she went?" Cole's sigh punched from his lungs and sounded more like a growl. "She's not protected by her connection to us. If she stays in too long, it could kill her! With no definite time within the portal to mature by, she could grasp any of the realm's timelines. And if she does make it to another plane, it will take hold of the related age and throw her body years ahead to catch up. Do you know what that does to a system?"

Rhune's voice held a touch of irritation. "You don't have to tell me. I saw it firsthand. Many of the colonists from Earth entered in their youth and came out geriatric."

The information set a knot in Vincent's gut, and he tried to think of a snarky response. The truth kept him silent. How often had she brought up the fact she was married to a Sentinel, a bearer of magic and wonder? Too often. Could she honestly believe being married to a Meridian would protect her as she walked the gateway to the realms? It was his fault if she did. He should have warned her, as Cole said.

Cole stood and looked at each of them in turn. "James, you go after Linda and the twins. Vincent run down Elaina. Rhune stay close. We'll need you for the Triad of Purpose if Kid doesn't make it back in time to close the portal. I'll prepare the globes for use within it as we leave Cornerstone Deep..."

As James stood, Cole realized his error in taking command and cringed. "I did it again. Apologies, brother. I had no right to place decision."

"I agree with your assessment."

Mianna held her hands out to her side. "What can I do to help?"

James heaved a sigh. "Prepare to console two very upset sisters. That is..." He glanced at Vincent. "If we're able to retrieve Elaina in time."

~ * ~

As Vincent grasped the edge of his cape, Rhune placed his hand on Vincent's arm. "She may not be in the portal, my boy. She may have made it to Midway. Find her before she's too weak and rush her back. Chances are, though, she's already reached that point." His cheeks seemed to melt as the man's countenance mellowed. "I pray she finds help in a server nearby. They have ways of getting her the energy she will need."

Unwilling to accept a dismal fate, Vincent shook his head. "Elaina is easily distracted. What happens in the gateway will no doubt do just that. I know she's still in there."

"Vincent, my boy..."

"No, Rhune. I need to focus on the portal."

Rhune sighed. "You won't find her in there, Vincentor."

With a snarl, Vincent turned, dispersing into the Smoke of Night. He barely heard his uncle's response as he darted out the study door. "Then the best action is to allow energy ripples to guide her. Show her the way. But you must be focused and patient."

Too much stood between him and the gateway to the realms; woodland, wildlife, the gravel tract to the foot of the granite bluff. Insects nettled him as he threw all his energy into the flight. Scenarios of the outcome cluttered his attempt to think of a way to help her, since he wouldn't be able to see her if she stood three paces ahead...

Would she be so lucky as to pass through the portal and not pause? If her pass wasn't immediate, she could cross over to Midway Summit ten, twenty, fifty years ahead of Cornerstone Summit's reckoning. Only the moment of thought mattered to carry the traveler to their destination. She could notice the shadows cast by her expelled energy and become confused, causing her to linger and affecting the time she emerged. What had Rhune said about guiding her with energy?

His disembodied senses noticed movement, and he glanced toward the far end of the landing. *Are those tents in the distance?*

Forgoing anything that would keep him from saving his love, he rushed forward. As the portal came into view, Vincent pushed harder, and called upon Midway Summit to open the gate. Bright light encircled the doorway, and as neon beams filled the center, he dashed into the white void.

Chapter Twenty-One

Wisps of clouds dispersed around James as he flew over the east countryside. Lanes of traffic stretch below, and he cursed the fact his scrying lens didn't work in a disembodied state. He made a pact to work on his mind reading skills when things settled down again. Focusing on cars with beige interiors, like what he saw in the Utopian's image when he performed the search, proved impossible. Between the speed of the vehicles, and his airborne point of view, he could make out very little.

He dipped and weaved among the traffic, opening his senses to catch bits of conversations in the vehicles as he passed over them.

This is fruitless!

Giving up on the strategy, he veered into a grove of birch trees on the side of the road and then materialized. He looked at his watch, and his voice punched from his throat. "Scry Jarrett Kilpatrick."

A scruffy face appeared over the lens of his watch, and James leaned his wrist until he caught sight of the color of the car. Off white? Beige...or gray? Did this guy ever clean his vehicle?

The location pulsed across his mind. He dispersed his elements into the Smoke of Night, and then darted toward the instructed destination far ahead. The off-white-beige-gray car of Jarrett Kilpatrick veered onto a side road, and James swooped to the driver's side. He pulled his essence together from the waist up, enough to enable him to speak, and allowed a tail of black smoke to swirl as the rest of his elements propelled him forward. He rapped on Jarrett's window.

The man jarred, and the car swerved as screams came from within.

"Oh, man, not *you*," yelled Jarrett.

Wind whipped Jarrett's straggly hair as James waved his hand to encompass the glass and it faded. "Pull this car over, or I'll do it for you!"

~ * ~

Cole stepped to the globes, took a deep breath to clear his lungs, and then released it as he rubbed his hands together. *Prepare the globes to seal Cornerstone Deep's gate to the realms. Forget the fact it was just opened, just released from a four-hundred-year separation from home.* The only thing to sage the thought was that he would be on the other side of the closed door this time. *With Mianna.*

A grin played on his lips. The Gods had known all along the part Mianna would play in the prophecy. And, being the ethereal beings they were, knew to prepare a backup in case he messed things up. *I sent her back to her first lifespan. Caused her to lose the experiences she'd gained to the point of being Anna. Oh, the curves life can throw. And oh to the mercy the Gods can show a romantic hearted Meridian Sentinel who would do anything to keep his love.*

He looked back at the globes, and his smile faded as he forced his mind to concentrate on the intricate layers needed to prepare the three Triad globes. Another deep breath and he focused. Elements in his mind's eye fell into place. The power of the image eased into the glowing balls.

If only Father had the time to perform the proper enchantments to seal the portal. He wouldn't have given his life's essence to complete the task. How different would life be if he had survived?

A part of him didn't want to know. He had Mianna, safe from Sylis Shilo's influence. He swallowed the bile in his throat at the fact his own father had longed for his wife and then pushed the topic aside.

Next step. Deep breath. Focus.

"Jamesuranton couldn't be making more of a disturbance out there."

Rhune's voice cut into Cole's concentration like a sword. He jarred, thoughts shattered before he could send them to alter the globes. Thank the Gods he wasn't in the middle of that.

Cole sent a glare over his shoulder to view Rhune at the cherry-wood desk. James' antics appeared over the mirrors of the Utopian in a miniature hologram. "If you're so concerned about how James is handling things, then why don't you go help him? You've just caused your own disturbance here. I need silence. The procedure could end in disaster if I focus on the wrong thing!"

"My apologies, Colhart." As Rhune stood, he took on the Smoke of Night and then darted out the door.

"Sorry, James," mumbled Cole. "But I'd say my task requires a Rhune free zone more than yours does."

Chapter Twenty-Two

Air rushed into Vincent's lungs as his body snapped into a whole state. He crumpled into himself and then remembered only solid souls may travel the gateway; the reason white flora carries those who have passed to their next life when in a foreign dimension. His determination doubled as he clenched his fists and stood. "Elaina!"

Small ripples followed the burst of air from his voice. The silence seemed to swallow the outcry into a muffled bubble. He gnashed his teeth together. How could he make such a disturbance as to guide his love back to safety before she entered Midway Summit? Or worse, before she slipped into the eternal sleep he'd learned of through Rhune's stories.

He grumbled. The best bet would be to get her to Midway and find a server to aid her until they could get back. That way, they'd at least have a few days to work with. Or could they even go back if she received energy assistance from someone living in another realm?

Logic slammed in his mind, and he tossed his hands out to his sides. What was he thinking? James had assigned him to help with the prophecy anyway. He was to take his mother's place if Rhune couldn't convince James to let Mechenzie train. This almost made Elaina's antic perfect. She'd be with him during his assignment. *Yes!*

His perspective renewed, Vincent dashed ahead, waving his arms and expelling as much energy as possible to create a disturbance for her to follow. Small thoughts of Midway littered his mind as to guide him closer to the plane.

No sign of Elaina within the white void.

A growl released nervous tension as panic seeped into his resolve. She could be anywhere in there. "*Elaina!*"

The wild shout sent distorted shadow in all directions. Spinning in a haphazard circle, he punched the emptiness with a charge of blue neon. The environment slowly warped it into shadow, and the band of power expanded out of sight.

"Midway Summit," Vincent said quickly, as to warp the circle into a path toward his destination. A tall doorway appeared in multicolored lights, and he stepped through to the other side.

Crisp splashes hammered in his ears, and he cringed, cupping his hands over his head. The noise of the waterfall slowly eased in his mind. Atmospheric electricity and beams of rainbow-colored light flashed within the liquid flow, and a light mist billowed from the rocks as water hit. Thick vines cast deep shadows over him in the concave behind a wide waterfall as the portal closed.

He'd been to the Midway dimension once in his life, and language, customs, and townships appeared in his mind like a dream. *This is Terrace Well. Father, Mother, and Uncle Rhune consecrated it for the gathering of the colonists. If Elaina made it this far...*

Vincent couldn't wait to clear the flow before he called for his love. "Elaina!"

He reached the sliver of space between water and rock in five long strides and then turned in a circle to take in the area at large. It looked as if the mountainside had opened its mouth to take a drink from the river, and foliage lined the soiled lips to spill from the opening. A deep cavern spread out across from the falls. "Gods, Elaina, if you're here, answer me!"

"Pwy ydych chi, obben?"

Jarred by the timid voice, Vincent spun to face an elderly man whose simple clothing shamed any vagabond on Terra. Loose fitting trousers reached his shins, and a tunic hung from one shoulder to draped him.

Vincent understood the foreign words as if he'd spoken them his whole life. It was a derivative of a language on Cornerstone Summit, one adopted by the settlers and their servants.

The man set his basket of fruit and leaves at his feet and looked as if he planned to kneel. He hesitated, meeting Vincent's gaze in a quick scan.

Vincent answered the man in his native tongue. "My name is Vincent. I'm looking for a woman who might have come through here."

"I am Amero." The man nodded and motioned toward a tunnel. "A Mistress, great with child. She was very weak, in need of service. She had no Talit to receive energy with, so I helped her to my master's abode, where the mistress there required service for her. But she is not well..."

Vincent shook his head. "That can't be the woman I'm looking for. Elaina isn't pregnant."

"Elaina?" He nodded with upped brows. "She pointed at herself and said Elaina Shilo many times."

~ * ~

Elaina clenched her fists and pressed her head into the soft pad of the cot. Energy surged in sporadic waves through her veins, and her hands and feet tingled to the point they felt like they could explode. She convulsed, each tremor threatening to knock the breath from her. The miracle within her stirred and added to the quakes shaking her body. How could the desire to have the child of the man she loved cause such physical confusion? She didn't know whether to sit, stand, or writhe on the cot they'd helped her onto. *Oh, dear stars! How did it come to this?*

And who were these people? Okay, they were kind strangers who took her in, but what kind of people had eyes that glimmered, skin pale as a baby's bottom, and spoke in such an odd tongue? *Why didn't I stop to think the people would speak a different language?*

The nurse jabbered beside her, her tiny lips fluttering illegible words. *Seriously, open your mouth wider and make some sense!* Elaina's exasperation exploded. "Will you just shut up? I can't understand you! I'm trying to calm down here, but the energy just won't stop, and your gibberish *isn't helping!*"

A tall man entered the room, his long fingers clutching a pad and pencil. The woman turned to him and shook her head. More jabbering from both this time. *Augh!*

The man stepped to the side of her bed, and his calm demeanor seemed to mock her state. "*Forstår du mig?*"

Elaina scoffed. "What?"

"*Me comprenez-vous?*"

Seriously? He's still trying to make me understand? "Huh?"

"*Verstehst du mich?*"

"Gods, you people are going to drive me crazy!" Elaina rolled her head to face the burnished rock wall. "Look," she said, turning to meet his gaze. "*I need my Goddess, Venus!*"

The woman's bushy brows jumped, and she placed her hand on the man's arm. "Venus?"

More gibberish. But she had understood the goddess's name. That's a good start!

"Yes, Venus! I need Venus."

The man nodded, but his frown told Elaina he wasn't happy. He placed his hand on his chest and then raised it toward the ceiling. "*Venus yn dduw.*"

Jitters punctuated Elaina's nod. "Yes, Venus is in heaven. But I need her. My husband... Vince, he could call on her. Can you find Vincent? He's a Sentinel. Is there a Sentinel here? Maybe he could reach her for me."

Turning away, the man shook his head. "*Dydy hi ddim yn deal, Hiedel,*" he said quietly and then sighed. "*Dim ond ceisiwch gadw ei chynhyrfu.*"

The woman nodded and picked up a damp cloth. As she placed it on Elaina's brow, the man walked from the room.

With a growl, Elaina threw her hands to her face. *Venus, you blessed me. Now please bless me again. I need... I need my Vince.*

Shilo Manor series~Destiny

Chapter Twenty-Three

James gnashed his teeth and spoke his command. "*Sitominus.*"

Cloaking spell in place, he clenched his fists, drew them upward, and the car lifted from the pavement.

Linda appeared beside Jarrett, her brows pulled tightly together, and cheeks flushed with her dropped jaw. "James. What are you doing? Please let me take my babies to a safe place!"

Jarrett swore under his breath. Linda dove over the back of the front seat, grabbing at the girls, and James shoved at the heavy machine. A flick of his finger, and the engine died as he gently placed the car on the shoulder of the road.

"You're not taking her, James," cried Linda. "She's my baby, can't you people understand that?"

As he turned for the door, she wedged herself between it and her twins.

James heaved a breath and lifted the latch. Of all the people Linda could have gone to for help, and she turned to Jarrett. Hadn't he proven to be a worthless husband, neglecting the well-being of his family? James sneered at the thought and then wrapped his arms around her waist and pulled her out of the car.

"James, *no!*"

James' biceps bulged as she fought against his hold. "Leenja, please. Believe me when I say I regret this course of action."

"Regret? You regret it? This is my child, my baby. I don't care if she's the God of Life herself. I'm her mother. Her *mother!*"

"Actually," came Rhune's voice in a soft tone. "She's the God of Light."

James sent a glare over his shoulder to find the man who brought this all on. "Don't you have somewhere to be?"

Rhune held up his hands. "I thought you might need a little help. Cole is readying the globes."

Ignoring the intrusion, James turned his attention back to Linda. "Nothing will stop you from being her mother, Leenja."

Linda's grip eased, but her body remained rigid. "So, I can go with her, and be there for her, and hold her when she needs me? I'll be there to see that she eats right, isn't forced to eat meat, and she'll have her sister, her *best friend*, there to cheer her on and support her in triumphs and failures?"

Closing his eyes, James pictured them

doing just that.

"Maybe we should let Mechenzie have a say in all of this," said Rhune. "She holds the soul who will ultimately have to decide whether or not to help in this situation."

Linda gripped James' arm so hard, her nails pierced his skin. "*What?* She's five years old."

"I'm six." The tiny voice broke into the throng and sounded foreign in the bustle of traffic and shouts. "And I want to help. I know who you're talking about. I mean I don't know them, but I do." Her little hand lighted on her chest, the same way it had the time James and Vince picked the girls up from their father's, and she spoke of the loved ones who had passed. "Something inside me says they need me, Momma."

Linda cut a warning glance at James and murmured. "Let me go to my child."

James slowly released her, and she knelt on the pavement in front of Mechenzie. Linda's elbows rested on the car seat as she took her daughter's hands in hers.

"Kenzie, this isn't like saving the butterflies or crickets from the birds. This could be very dangerous."

"But you and Mandy will be there, won't they Poppa James? And Uncle Rhune won't let anything happen to me. I know he won't."

"I will do everything in my power to keep her safe." Rhune couldn't have sounded more sincere.

And James hated him for it. He muffled a growl. *No doubt he will. So he can claim her as soon as she matures.*

A heavy sigh issued from Linda's lips, and she peered at Rhune over her shoulder. "Only, and I repeat, *only* if Mandy and I are able to be with her during all of this."

Jarrett threw his arm over the back of his seat. "What about me?"

Straightening, James glared at him. "What about you?"

Jarrett turned around and disappeared somewhere on the other side of the driver's seat.

James lowered to one knee and stroked Linda's cheek with his thumb. "Leenja, you don't realize how things work on Meridian. There will be many times she will be in deep meditation; no one other than the instructor may be present."

"Well..." Linda nodded a jerky bob. "That's different."

"And her instructor would be someone close to the situation."

"It would be you right, James? I mean, you're her new father. You're as close as it gets. Right?"

"No, my Terran Tiger Lily," said Rhune. "I'm as close as it gets."

"Well..." Linda's hands fumbled around Mechenzie's. "As long as we're there."

Pinching the bridge of his nose, James released a low sigh. "Leenja. Souls from a cornerstone realm may not survive for as long as it could take to complete her training."

He wasn't about to lose them to Linda's stubbornness, but how in the Arched Spectrum of Realms could he be the one to crush his love's heart by separating her family? She was right not to trust him. James saw that now.

~ * ~

Voices barged into Cole's concentration as he lifted his hands before the three globes. He bunched his fingers into fists. Two more steps, and they couldn't be more crucial. He angled a glance over his shoulder to view the door.

Rhune's tenor carried over Linda's alto cord. "I'm all for the mother being with her child, but we can't allow Terrans to live in Champaign, Meridian. A visit is one thing, but this will take time, Jamesuranton."

"I'm going to be with my baby," Linda shouted.

Cole imagined James lifting his hand as he spoke. "We're not only talking of her mother, Rhune. There's Mandy."

"Hey now," came a stranger's voice. "What about me?"

A trio of voices met the man's question. "Shut up, Jarrett."

Silence.

Someone sighed.

"Look. The Terrans can't live in our dimension. The energy flow is too different. Midway Summit alone drains the life from them."

James responded. "You gave the gift of life to the colonist from Earth. You could do the same for them."

"That was for life on Moraine, Midway Summit. I can't extend it to Champaign unless the soul is Meridian, such as for Mechenzie. They wouldn't last a week. And the gift of life may not protect a child from the differences in the Spectrum's position. The heat alone will be difficult to bear."

"You would love to have Mechenzie to yourself back home. Admit it. All of this goes to your planning."

"You read me wrong, son." Rhune's voice softened, "Lilith and I are soul mates, yes. But I would never influence her to decide, especially before she was ready. Her soul must decide such things. What is

206

special about a coerced love? How could both grow if one manipulates the other?"

Cole stepped to the door and peeked around the jamb. The group came to view in the foyer down the hall, and if he read the expressions right—and he knew he did through his telepathy—the comment softened James' regard somewhat. His brother's thoughts hit Cole strong, and he smiled, his view changing with James' understanding. *He didn't want to keep her to himself? To groom her for when he could claim her as his bride?*

"You called me son."

"What?"

"Rhune, you called me son."

"You are my son, Jamesuranton. And will always be. I don't want to harm Mechenzie."

James lowered his gaze, and Rhune held his hands out to his sides. "Look, training Mechenzie on Champaign, Meridian, has its advantages on many levels. But as we are called to serve a mission on Midway Summit, allow me to train her there. I can bless the family, and with the Counsel's permission, they can join us."

Cole's brows jumped. *Indeed.*

Rhune looked at James and Linda in turn. "Is that agreeable?"

James' regard softened to the point Cole thought he might embrace the man. "That is very agreeable. Leenja?"

Quick nods bounced the blonde hair around her shoulders. "As long as we're together, I don't care where we go."

Jarrett lifted his finger and took a step sideways. "Let me get this straight. We're going to another dimension? As in an alternate existence? What does that mean? Are there strange creatures? Food? Will there be beer?"

Cole snorted.

"There are equivalents of everything, my boy," said Rhune. "And as it so happens, our little Terran butterfly and Vincentor have already passed through the portal."

James straightened. "You mean he hasn't returned yet? How could you not go after her to offer the Gift of Life? Time shifts within the portal. You don't know how long she's been in there!"

"Oh, your father designed ways around the receiving of my gift. I'm certain she's been served and they're safe within the walls of Moraine's Shilo Manor."

"Rhune you don't know that."

"I was following your instructions, Jamesuranton. You asked that I stay to fill the Triad."

James set his hands at his waist. "I fully expected Vince to have returned by now." He looked at the cascading chandelier as if weighing his decision. "Go. Go find them, make sure Elaina is safe. And with the situation with the portal escalating, keep them there. It will save us time."

"I shall make haste." With a smile, Rhune flourished his cape and dispersed into the Smoke of Night. As he darted out the door, it swung closed behind him.

Jarrett sidestepped again, as if to gain the others' view. "No, really. Do they have beer?"

Chapter Twenty-Four

Shadows danced along the wide catacomb as Amero's hand wobbled with each step. How the old man managed to hold the thick braded torch handle with his gnarled fingers was beyond Vincent, and how these people managed to live in a world beneath rock, he didn't know. Then again, he studied the crystal-lighted torch. *How did they get a crystal to produce light?* The large gem, positioned in an intricate cap at the top of the handle, glowed bright. For such a rugged environment, the thing looked very refined.

Amero passed the light to his other hand as they maneuvered an incline. He gingerly selected the easiest path as his thin slippers slid on the rubble. Vincent thanked the gods he wore boots.

As they came to a T in the pass, Amero veered right. Five more strides brought them to a small tunnel on the left. The man paused and peeked at Vincent from shy eyes. He lowered his head as he spoke quietly. "Are you an Allant? You look very much like one."

The last thing Vincent needed was to cause premature concern or veneration.

Aside from the fact he wasn't one of the actual High Ones, he hated the title. No one should set themselves above another, no matter the dimension they're from. How his father could push for such an arrangement was beyond him. "My name is Vincent."

The man's gaze shot to the ground, and he flushed. "I am Amero."

"Yes, I think you mentioned that. Thank you for your help, Amero. Out of curiosity, why would you think I'm a High One?"

To show he knew the meaning of the word Allant could only help the man feel more comfortable in his presence, and perhaps get him to see Elaina quicker.

"The stories tell of the Allants returning one day with black hair, eyes like onyx, and..." he motioned with his torch. "Your fists have a light of red that deepens when you make them tighter."

Vincent looked at the tell-tale sign of his tension and heaved a sigh. *Okay. Check yourself, Vince. We don't need this kind of attention.*

"Right. Well, my hands do feel very warm. But my name is Vincent, and I'm looking for my wife."

"If you are not an Allant, and your eyes do not shimmer like a master, then are you from the World of the Sun?"

Vincent glanced to the side. *Master?*

Right. Rhune had said something about the people of the world below practicing slavery. So Amero was no doubt a slave. It was the only thing that could explain his poor clothing. He stifled a sneer at the thought. If these people must work in the rock, why not provide more suitable shoes, in the least? "Yes, a world where I live in the sunshine."

"So, you are her server, searching for your mistress."

"I'm looking for my *wife*."

The man's brows dipped as his lips parted, and he seemed to struggle to understand. "You...you mated with your..." He quickly cleared his throat, wiped his hand down his tunic.

"My wife and I are not servants nor masters. We're free and love each other."

Amero nodded. Lifting his gnarled hand, he motioned toward the small tunnel. "She is in there."

As they dipped into the small pass, the torch bleached the sediment white. Silver shale tiled a narrow door and glowed in the bright light from the crystal. Rollers rumbled on a track, and the thin slabs clattered against each other as Amero slid the closure aside.

An oval room appeared beyond the threshold, lit to the brightness of high noon. Burnished amber made up the walls, floor, and a small staircase that led to a second landing balcony. Alabaster seating huddle to the right, while two arched hallways took up the left side of the room. A small cabinet stood at the far end, and another took up the space beside the shale door. A wide cylinder with several garments lying across it filled a nook under the steps. Crystals, much like the one in Amero's torch, lined the tapering ceiling. For being underground, Vincent noted the warmth of the place, but he couldn't find the source of the heat. *Now this is the way to camp underground.*

"I will get the mistress," said Amero as he bustled down hallway number one.

Vincent ran his fingertips along the smooth rock wall. *This is an amazing feat to accomplish in a cavern.* He touched the white cabinet beside him. Smooth rock. *Maybe these people aren't so bad off after all.*

Footsteps sounded from the other hall, and Vincent turned to greet the people. As they entered the main room, three more servants, dressed in brown tunics, looked at him and then halted. They dropped to their knees, sitting on their feet, and placed their hands on the floor, bowing their heads low.

Vincent waved his hand. "You don't have to do that."

"Then perhaps it should be you who bows along with them."

The soprano in the voice couldn't have been older than twelve, but the command in the tone suggested this young woman was used to throwing her slight weight around. Vincent peered over his shoulder and frowned at the young lady seated in one of the chairs. Definitely no older than twelve. *Was she there all along?* "And you are?"

She lifted her dainty chin. "Becca Compton, and this is Master Almadore's abode."

"I'm only looking for my wife. I was told she was brought here by the man at the falls. Amero."

"Amero?" The youth's blue eyes shifted to the side, and Vincent caught an odd shimmer in her irises. "Amero assists in gathering the healing supplies and settling new arrivals. I wasn't aware Rawkin acquired a new slunk maid, much less a set."

Vincent placed his hands at his waist. "He hasn't. Elaina is my wife, and I'm here to take her home."

With a shake of her head, the young woman stood and then folded her arms. "If you weren't a suitable mate, she'll be assigned another."

"Suitable mate? Young lady, you don't know what you're talking about. Where's this Master Almadore?"

She scoffed. "My father is a Leading Father of the Nation. I'd say I know what I'm talking about concerning servers."

A lanky boy, about the same age, peeked from the tunnel behind the bowed servants. "I thought you were talking again before you figured things out." He placed his hands at the sides of his waist and stood tall. "He's no slunk. One look at how he stands proves that. He shows pride."

Vincent huffed.

Becca's gaze flew over Vincent as she scowled. "Well, his eyes don't shimmer."

The boy snorted. "How can you tell? They're black." As if that ended the conversation, he added a command to the slaves. "Shelle, Drake, Elise, rise and return to your duties."

He motioned with his nod and then strode into the neighboring hall. "Your wife is in the healer's room. When she got here, we were confused at her state. She was talking in some odd language and very weak. With her condition, we couldn't just leave her on her way. Rawkin's Terrace Well abode is the only one for at least a mile. It's

216

a good thing he and Father had business and brought the medical staff to check the servers. If she came and only the slunks were here, they'd be afraid to deal with her." He glanced Vincent's way. "None would want to view her in her state for fear of shaming her. Rawkin's slaves are among the best trained, you know."

"Ah," Vincent said, not understanding at all.

"Of course, if they could have understood her, they would have rendered service immediately."

A knot set in Vincent's gut. He hadn't considered her inability to communicate with the natives of Midway Summit. If the portal had aged her at all, she would definitely be in a weakened state when she emerged. If the servants would have indeed ignored her for fear of their master's rebuke, he owed Amero a huge service. Perhaps his belief of the return of the High Ones had aided in his decision to help. He'd obviously witnessed the lights of the portal when she emerged. *Thank you, Amero, for not ignoring her plight.*

As they turned into another oblong room, Elaina's cry pierced his heart.

"Vince! Oh, Gods, Vince, it's you!" Her back arched, legs shook, and body trembled beneath the thick blankets draped over her on the small cot. She appeared to have difficulty holding her hands to her chest, and her head jarred in spams as if convulsions controlled her.

He rushed to her side and then took her hands in his to steady them. "Gods, Elaina," he whispered. "What have they done to you?"

Sharp jitters punctuated her tremors, and tiny squeaks rode her breaths. "No, V-Vince. It was V-Venus..."

A tall man entered, holding a pad and pencil, and walked directly to Vincent. "Do you understand me?

"Yes, of course. What's happened to my wife?"

"So, you know her. Good. I'm Doctor McGroy. We've tried several times to find the language she speaks. We even attempted what we knew of the ancient tongues."

"No, she's from very far away. We've just come here and she...wandered off."

The doctor shook his head. "She shouldn't be traveling in her condition. The last time I saw this..." he peeked over his shoulder to the young man and then lowered his voice. "Do you trust your servers Mr...?"

"Shilo. Vincent Shilo. And I, uh...I trust those who are with us explicitly."

"Oh." The man's gaze fitted to his, and then he did a double take. "Oh. I see. When she acquired service, it was almost too much for her. I gave her a sedative to help her rest," the doctor whispered so low Vincent could barely make out the words.

"It doesn't seem to be working very well."

"She is much calmer than she was, Mr. Shilo. I'm afraid she will suffer like this for the rest of her pregnancy, which by the look of things, won't be much longer."

Vincent looked at the pile of thick blankets. With Elaina's feet pulled close to her bottom and her knees pointed at the ceiling, could the covers really be hiding a... "Pregnancy?"

"Ah, yes." The doctor's brow furrowed, and he scanned Vincent's face with shimmering eyes. "You are her husband and are unaware?"

Vincent's blood rushed to his head. *The man is serious?* He whipped the covers from Elaina's body. Her belly, round with child, seemed to glare at him with reproach. *Oh my...Gods! It's true.*

The man took Vincent's arm and led him a few feet away. "I see this is a surprise. And it is entirely possible that she withheld this information from you until it was no longer possible. Perhaps the reason she fled?" The pad teetered in his hand. "Of course, you know the consequences of mating with a mistress, mister. This drastic condition doesn't happen when the father is...of pure blood."

The accusation in the doctor's voice screamed trouble, and Vincent didn't need a reason to lose his temper among these people. Not now with the return of the Allants at hand. If they considered him a servant and not of pure blood, would they keep him from her? Arrest him for crossing the line between master and slave?

Wrenching his arm from the man's grip, Vincent marched to Elaina, bent, and scooped her into his arms. Turning, he marched past Dr. McGroy, bumping him aside, and dipped into the long hallway. Before anyone could follow, he dispersed their elements into the Smoke of Night, careful to include the delicate contents of her womb.

He darted down the hall, through the foyer, and then thinned their essences as he aimed for the small space beneath the shale door of the abode. They emerged into the darkness of the narrow tunnel, and Vincent used his senses to avoid the walls and boulders on the way. Whipping left at the T, he flew at full force to get as much space between them and the underground dwellers as possible.

The scent of damp sediment and iron penetrated his senses as they passed the Terrace Well waterfall and flew upward, out of the giant opening in the mountainside. Hot rays from the white sun cast bright light on the lush valley ahead, and Vincent paused to remember the layout of the great hills surrounding the Midway Summit Shilo Manor. Languages and customs had come easily, but which way to the Shilo Manor that stood in shadow?

Elaina's elements pulsed with energy, and he realized how drastic her symptoms were. How did all this happen? Would his seed really cause such a reaction to a woman born of another dimension? For that matter, how could the gods choose to grant him a child when his soul had only begun the course of eternal life? He hadn't experienced enough to be a father! So many Meridian couples prayed for this blessing, and he and Elaina were chosen? Could her pleas have reached Venus, and in mercy the Goddess consorted with Taravaughn, the God of Life of Cornerstone Deep, and granted the prayers? *It's unbelievable!*

Vincent pushed aside the questions to tackle the issue at hand. He focused on their surroundings. Mountain peaks and valleys appeared on every side. But he knew they were west of the white orchard that homed the Sentinels' manor. Keeping to the mountain top, he headed east in hopes he'd spot the apricot trees from a distance.

Pines stretched high, framing gray bluffs so tall they put the ones on Cornerstone Deep to shame. Seagulls sang long chords beside them, no doubt claiming Sheridan Sea to the rear as their home.

Fields of clover broke into the woodland, and Vincent had to wonder if the people harvested the crop for some reason, or if honey was the goal. Regardless, the purple flora broke the wide variety of greenery beautifully.

A squirm produced a nauseating wave through his senses, and reality hit him again. There was a third life connected to his essences. His offspring. His child. Was it safe to be traveling by Smoke of Night with an unborn infant? *Come on, Vince, find that manor.*

A vast city spread out to the right, one he'd never thought possible on a plane so young. Tall buildings glistened in the bright sunlight, motored transport sped along wide lanes of paved road, and he couldn't help comparing it to Shilo City. So many unknowns lay ahead. So many changes. And so many questions.

Chapter Twenty-Five

The bright light of the portal passed in a flash as Rhune stepped into the door and emerged behind the waterfall on Midway Summit. He lifted his cloak against the mist and cursed the wet rocks as his thin shoes got soaked.

A boy's voice punctuated the noisy splashes and caught Rhune's attention with a jerk. He turned to the sliver of space between the rock and the waterfall as the lad ran to a man beyond the flow. "Obu! Another light flashed from behind the falls!"

Warped bodies moved beyond the flux of streaming water, and Rhune pressed his lips together with a sigh. *Another light? These people have noticed the portal's activity.*

"Hurry," said an elderly man as he handed the boy a bundle. "Get these herbs to Master Almadore. They are needed quickly."

"Yes, Obu."

Having not heard the word used for father in so many years, Rhune had to smile. *I've always liked that word. Obu.*

The youngster wrapped his arms around the satchel and then darted out of sight. A woman's form leaned to the man, and Rhune barely made out her words above the din.

"What does this mean, Amero? Are the High Ones returning?"

"I do not know. The man who entered before did not look like the one who came to us twelve years ago." He took a few steps closer to the falls and seemed to look beyond the water toward Rhune. "There is somebody in there."

As the obu's head leaned into the sliver of space, he called to Rhune. "Are you all right? Do you require service?"

A heavy hand slapped Rhune on the shoulder from behind, and he spun to face a Senior Sentinel of the Spectrum of Realms. His dark hair hugged his scalp, plastered with sheen until small waves curled around the back of his thick neck. The indigo jacket he wore couldn't hide his muscular form, and Rhune grinned at how closely they matched his own. How many times had people back home on Meridian commented on how they looked like brothers? Rhune had lost count. But the man definitely held his youthful features well. Slight wrinkles creased his forehead and eyes, his thin brows pressed tightly above the bridge of his narrow nose. Perhaps he had served in a foreign dimension that would allow him to age slowly.

The base in the man's voice rumbled in response to Obu's query. "Oh, he is *not* all right."

"Zacharius, I—"

The man dispersed into the Smoke of Night, forcing Rhune's body to do the same with his touch. He shot upward through crevices, and then left the wide mouth in the side of the mountain, carrying Rhune with him.

A bright sky and white sun met them in contrast to the misted shadows. Heat penetrated Rhune's essence, such a welcome change from the constant cold of the Cornerstone Deep realm. But why the rude approach from the well-known Sentinel? He was, after all, following the wishes of the council by getting involved with Midway Summit again.

Zipping along the countryside, he allowed Zacharius to lead. The timberland stretched tall in the mid-northern territory and looked like spikey hair growing from the rolling toes of the great mount. Fields of blue and purple flowers unfolded in large patches to the right, while the western horizon gleamed with the crests of Sheridan Sea. They merged left, and Rhune recognized the course they took immediately; the route to Shilo Manor.

Small townships nestled within the woodland, cattle grazed in valleys, and as orchards took over the view, white flora dominated the treetops.

Snuggled within the arbors at the foot of the mountain, Shilo Manor stood, not in shadow as Rhune had expected, but clearly a mansion of high worth. Perhaps Vincent found the home and released it from its slumber. That would explain the brilliant scene. Though Zacharius' presence placed question to that theory. But why would the Sentinel be here?

Zacharius' hold tightened on Rhune's elements, and he dipped toward the manor. The front door flew wide.

As they materialized in the foyer, the man rounded on Rhune with a scowl. "Over four hundred years. *Four hundred years,* I've been assigned here with the meager development these people have made. And when you decide to return, you send a woman from a Cornerstone Realm like the others. She didn't even speak the language! She was lucky there were servants near the well at the time because I was *not* about to get involved with another one of your stunts. And that's another thing. Servers saw her come from behind the portal falls!"

He tossed his hand through the air. "And then a clueless Meridian enters this dimension. *Both* unannounced. *Both* making contact with the inhabitants beneath the rock before I can make contact with them."

"That was Elaina, a sweet Terran, but naïve of the consequences of her actions. And he is Sylisan's son, Vincentor. She is his wife. He simply came after her."

The man's face turned red and the veins in his neck swelled. He pointed to the way they came. "She partook of the energy of a server to survive, Rhune! She'll never be allowed to leave!"

Rhune's sigh rumbled in his throat. "Ah, well, there are a few things you should know about the return of the High Ones. Things have become a little more complicated."

He glanced around the sparse hall. Cherubim lined the walls of the foyer, just as they had in all the Shilo Manors, but the special touches Lilith had brought to the one on Cornerstone Deep weren't a part of this house. It was definitely a bachelor's abode, and Rhune could imagine the women having a time with redecorating. Especially Colhart's little Terran angel. "Tell me, Zacharius, where is the young couple? I expected them to have found their way here by now."

"The last time I checked the Utopian, they were headed this way via the highlands."

"A difficult point of view to find the manor, especially if you're not familiar with the area. I'll go after them." He looked at his watch and called up the scry. The luminescent face throbbed as he spoke. *"Bhiorus, Vincentor Shilomacj."*

Vincentor's essence appeared over the face of the instrument as the Smoke of Night, and Rhune widened the view to gather where to find him. A large city expanded to the right, the mountain side to his left. Ahead lay a quaint ferry crossing.

"That's near Carter's Cross," said Zacharius. "It's been the target of several incidences. They don't need to interfere there, Rhune." The man placed his hand on Rhune's arm and lowered his chin, accentuating his point. *"You* don't need to interfere there. Just go get them and return immediately. This world doesn't need the influence of outsiders, whether you mean well or not."

Rhune cleared his throat. He knew what Zacharius referred to, and he didn't blame him one bit. With a nod, he dispersed his elements into the Smoke of Night.

Chapter Twenty-Six

Cole glowered at the Utopian as he watched the activity in the hologram above the mirrors. *How arrogant and self-serving this dimension is. How can they possibly believe no harm will come of their meddling?*

By the light of a full moon, several men slowly neared the sheer bluff beside the boulder that had dropped during the fight with Dressen. *They get no closer to the portal.* "James, get in here now!"

Footsteps rumbled down the hall as what seemed like the whole group responded to his call. They filed into the hallowed study, including a blond-streaked stranger—who could only be Jarrett—and then clambered around the desk. Cole nodded at the dark picture above the tulip-shaped stage of mirrors.

James' brows bit together as he scanned the scene. "They're at the portal. I'll go. You get those globes ready."

He turned, and as a dark mist overtook him, he added a direct thought to Cole's mind. *"Watch the girls for me."*

Cole glanced at Linda and then watched the scene play out in the hologram.

"He said it was to the right," said a man in the image. "Sir Vincent was defending it."

Lord Carrington and his oversized mouth. Cole's glower deepened.

"Lord Dressen had to have made it open," said another. "The wizards wouldn't have done it, not knowing he wanted to get through."

"Maybe it only shows if you say something they would say. Sound...magical."

One of them scoffed at the same time Cole did.

"No, really. Say something."

"Like what?" The man's voice turned deep and mocking, "I command you to open!"

Linda's cheek quirked.

"No, like...*bhiorus.*"

"Where did you learn that?"

"I overheard Sir Vincent once when he searched for a harvest subject."

Linda leaned her curves over the desk to peer past Jarrett. "They can't open it just like that, can they?"

Cole shook his head. "Only if you..."

As if one of the men had read Cole's mind, he finished his sentence. "Speak the name of where you want to go. Like where they're from. Yeah. Meridian."

White lines traced the tall arch of the doorway to the realms. As the center melted away, an array of multicolored neon lights beamed through the rock.

Blood drained from Cole's face, Linda covered her mouth with her fingers, and Jarrett cheered.

Everyone looked at him.

"What? It's cool, right? Just look at it!"

Cole's command punched the air. "Linda, you and the girls grab only what you can carry to take with you to Midway Summit. I'll get that spell ready now!"

Linda rushed out of the study with the girls, and Jarrett twirled in all directions. "What about me? What should I do?"

Cole scowled at the man. "Go home."

His blue gaze locked onto Cole's. "I can't go home. My golden girls are all I have in the world. My home is nothing without them! If they're going to live in some other dimension, I'm going with them. Dad said it himself; those girls have a right to have their father in their lives. I may not be worth much, Sir Shilo, but I have a right to have them in mine too."

A grimace twitched on Cole's lips. Whether he liked it or not, the words struck a chord in Cole's heart. The man was right. But another Terran soul on Midway? He could always perform a partial memory sweep, but with children involved he'd have to go deep into the man's psyche. He shuffled his feet as he squared his shoulders. *The children.* They did deserve to have their father in their lives.

With a heavy sigh, Cole raked his fingers through his hair. *If the gods allow it, then so may it be. James is really going to love this one.* "If you have nothing, then I guess you'll be packing light."

~ * ~

As James reached the bluff landing, he formed his upper body to allow breath. Gnashing his teeth with his snarl, he pulled his dark essence to billow around him, creating an ominous sight for the men to behold. He filled his lungs with salty sea air and bellowed as one brave—or stupid—soul stepped into the white void. *"Halt!"*

Their gazes whipped to see him. Jaws dropped, and eyes opened wide.

James drew his hand through the air, and wind whirled. Rubble rose and bulleted their bodies. They backed behind the boulder for safety.

James formed between them and the gateway to the realms and waved his hand at the face of the bluff. The door closed.

"*What* do you think you're *doing*? To enter this portal is a breach of the covenant!"

"Wait, Lord Travis is in there!"

With a shake of his head, James looked at the man. He let the grave tone in his voice speak of the finality of the act. "Lord Travis is gone. If he reaches Meridian, he'll not be allowed entry and turned away, lost to roam the portal the rest of his days. All noblemen know the consequences of a breach such as this."

Stepping into a wide turn to face the portal, James gathered his energy. *Let's show them who they're messing with.*

His arms bulged as he commanded the rubble to create a blockade before the face of the bluff. His growl accompanied the upward motion of his fists, and his chest expanded, shoulders arched. His biceps grew twice their size as he commanded a protective shield to warp over the barricade. A thick opalescent sheen expanded over the blocked portal, and James shoved at the air before him. The protectant shield rammed into the bluff, causing pebbles to clatter to the landing.

He wheeled toward the men. "Because of the selfish designs of the noblemen, this portal is to be closed. The Gods have spoken. The Sentinels have been called to serve elsewhere, and Cornerstone Deep will be dead to the Arched Spectrum of Realms until the Gods Taravaughn, Gryffin, and Arylin deem it worthy to reopen. Pray for mercy! You have defiled that which was sacred!"

Furling his cloak before his face, James allowed his angry black eyes to be the last view of him the men would see. He dispersed his elements and shot toward Shilo Manor. *Foolish, foolish souls.*

Should he have attempted to help Lord Travis find his way back? A screeching roar sounded through the arbors, and his senses soured. The answer came clear as Gryffin spoke directly to his heart and mind. *"The laws are clear. The door must be sealed."*

Chapter Twenty-Seven

Vincent flew low along the woodland harboring the peaks of the mountain. Several small tracts with camping sites appeared among the trees, but none promised a haven to rest so he could assess Elaina's condition. Her elements flew along with his, content, serene. Given her state in the caves, Vincent had to wonder how. His nerves edged on exasperation.

Then it hit him. She'd opened so fully to him again, he'd taken on her excess of energy. *Whatever makes her more comfortable is my duty at this point. My sweet Elaina, the mother of my child, I'll forever seek your comfort and joy.*

As he rounded a gorge, a lakeside ferry tethered to a pier came to view. A boathouse neighbored the long boardwalk, and a small shack sat in a grove a few yards away. Families filed from the barge, cheer evident in their laughter. Children romped on the sturdy planks as fathers donned packs no doubt used during the trip. Waves rushed up the sandy shore and crashed into the small bluff not far from the party goers. Sprays shot high onto a cave landing and drizzled down the steep rocky foundation.

Nausea washed through Vincent's essence, and Elaina's condition rushed back to him. *Right. Find a place to rest.*

As he dipped beside the rugged shack, he pulled their elements together with her in his arms. Tremors overtook her body again, and he quickly scooted around the corner to enter the little abode. He barely registered the sign on the door that read Carter's Cross.

For such a rugged look, the modest home seemed comfortable enough: bed, settee, tripod table with chairs, and the equivalent of a stove and basin. The people seemed advanced enough to have indoor plumbing and lighting.

As he quickly laid Elaina on the bed, a chorus of screams erupted from outside. He peeked past the door and blinked twice to pull together the scene. Golden beams shot through the air, hit the travelers, and returned in a heartbeat. A man nearby grasped his chest, gasped, and then fell to the ground with a groan.

Vincent scanned the area for the cause. His disbelief passed his lips in a mumble. "I didn't know they had advanced weapons here."

"It's called a Talit. And they aren't

weapons."

Rhune's voice caused Vincent to choke on his breath, and he wheeled around to face the man. "How long have *you* been here?"

"As soon as we got our Linda squared away, I thought you could use some help. I got to the manor expecting to find you there, but alas, you and the Terran butterfly hadn't made it. I scryed for you and surmised you were lost, my dear boy."

Vincent glowered. "Never mind that. What's going on out there?"

"I'd hazard to say the deep dwellers have surfaced. Those beams look much like the ones Sylisan created to help a portion of the settlers who branched off into the caverns. They refused to believe in the mixing of blood."

"Mixing of blood?"

"They insisted on keeping their bloodlines pure, and as such, refused the Gift of Life I offered."

Right. He did mention that along with the prophecy. As much as Vincent wanted to know more, he turned his attention to Elaina, writhing on the bed, but couldn't ignore the activity outside. "Okay, so they're the deep dwellers. How do we stop them from hurting these people without calling attention to ourselves?"

"Well, that, my boy, is a question suited for a Head of Sentinels. We're to observe and keep the natives from the portal while not influencing their ways. This is their domain."

"You mean do nothing?"

"I mean, mind our own business and get your lovely wife to the safety of Shilo Manor. While you've been wasting time, she's suffering. I had no idea she carried your child. It looks like she lingered a short time in the portal and it accelerated the growth."

Spasms punctuated her pleas. "Help me. Vince...please, help me."

Vincent spun on his heels and faced his love. Her tremors had turned to sharp jolts, and he reached her in one long step. Kneeling before her, he let his hand hover, afraid to touch her. How delicate was the child? How gentle must he be? *A father. I'm to be a father! Of a living breathing child that Elaina and I made. What do I do?*

"My boy, if you don't scoop her into your arms and fly, I'm about to. She needs attention best shown to her in Shilo Manor."

Ignoring his insecurities, Vincent gently wrapped his arms around Elaina. "It's okay, Elaina. We'll get you help."

Her breath puffed against his neck.

"Help...me."

Sweet Gods! He took on the Smoke of Night the same time Rhune did and followed his uncle as he darted out of the little shack.

Midway Summit Shilo Manor looked surreal as it loomed on a large mound off the mountainside. White blossoms crowned the arbors that surrounded the ancient home like a blanket of snow. They were obviously the white flora, prepared to accompany Meridian souls to their next lives, a prominent part of the Sentinel tools. He'd come to cherish the bright beautiful petals, despite the reminder of their duties to them.

Darting over the front lawns, Vincent's senses sighed in relief. The door flew wide, and as they entered, Rhune halted.

Vincent scattered his and Elaina's essence to keep from flowing through the jumble of molecules and then scoffed to himself. He'd felt his uncle's strong presence the entire way. No need to try to avoid him. As he billowed to gain control, he noticed the reason for the sudden stop.

A man who looked much like Rhune in stature, excelled in what must be the area's fashion of the time—sheened hair, indigo jacket, and black shoes to match his trousers. His set jaw didn't look inviting, and Vincent wondered what had gone wrong to cause the stern look.

A second man wore dark blue, and his outfit mimicked a military hero—badges, clips, pins; they all adorned his collar, arms, and breast. His hands tucked at the crook of his arms, the man lifted his clean-shaven chin to peer at them with dark eyes.

Vincent took solid form the same time Rhune did, and Elaina's weight pulled downward on his arms. He tightened his hold.

Rhune greeted the man to their left. "Zacharius, who is this? I tell you of a confidential situation, and you contact a local?"

Zacharius' deep voice filled the receiving hall with little effort as he shook his head. "This is High Admiral Hilton. In accordance with our agreement with the nobles of Midway Summit, a spokesman has been notified of the breach. This affects their people. I'm sure you remember the last time this happened, Rhune. The gods refused help, and you stepped in. He doesn't want a repeat of the effect it had on his world."

Vincent sneered at the obvious disregard for the crying woman in his arms. "This is my wife, and she carries my child. She will get help whether any of you are ready for it or not."

Rhune held up his large hand, and Vincent rolled his jaw, ready to rebuke. But Elaina's jittery voice sounded beside his ear. "Venus. Venus...blessed us...with this...child. The Gods have found...favor with us."

The man to their right dipped his brows into a deep furrow. "Are you telling me my Goddess allows your entry into our dimension? That she sanctifies this breach after her willingness to let the others die for seeking worlds beyond their own?"

"If you'll recall your history, High Admiral," said Rhune. "Those colonists sought for riches and eternal youth. They were selfish in their search. Elaina here desires to give her husband a family. A blessing the Goddess Venus dearly loves to grant."

Zacharius held his hands to his sides and spoke to the Admiral. "There has been no contact from the gods. Positive or otherwise. If they condemned the entry into their world, I would have heard of it by now. I have, however, heard from the counsel of Meridian. I'm to be replaced by a Triad of Sentinels."

He didn't think it possible, but the General's brow furrowed deeper. "A triad?"

Rhune stepped toward him as he

nodded. "Three that act on behalf of the Gods when needed. High Admiral, the prophecy is about to come to pass. As I replace Zacharius, I'll see to it your world will only change for the better."

"For the better? Under whose terms? What's better to you could bring chaos to Moraine. These changes will pass through me and my trusted advisors first. I expect to be counseled on everything that happens and have say in such happenings. You will take the place of Zacharius at the university and be monitored regularly."

Rhune nodded. "I'm aware of his contribution to ancient studies. I'm an excavator in my own right and am willing to take his position."

A burst of exasperation rattled in Elaina's chest, and Rhune quickly turned his attention to her. "But now, if I may, this young lady requires attention. Vincent, my boy, lead the way to your new room. I'll do my best to prepare her. She's in for a trying delivery."

Delivery.

Reality hit Vincent anew. Of all the things that could have happened, he never expected this. Did Venus really intervene? Or was it the phenomenal love making session while in Smoke of Night that brought them this miracle? Every fiber of his being had burned with their joined climax. Every molecule had sought her satisfaction, and he had felt every particle of her open to him.

In an instant, Vincent dispersed their elements and then darted to the third-floor master suite. Elaina's emotions melded with his, and he realized how frightened she'd become. No doubt the acceleration of gestation caused shock, and now she faced an experience she was ill prepared for. Hoping and praying didn't account to knowing and preparing for the moment.

He gently laid her on the bed and then pulled their essences into solid form. Her scream tore at his heart.

"Vince, I can't take it anymore! I feel like I'm on *fire*. The baby... Oh, sweet Venus, help me!"

Rhune materialized beside him and quickly cupped Elaina's face with his large hands. "Elaina, everything is going to be fine."

"What's *happening*? Why do I feel like my veins are going to *explode*?"

"You carry the child of a Meridian man, my little Terran butterfly. Your body is from a dimension with a much slower...metabolism."

A kind way to say their minds and bodies weren't as advanced, and Vincent appreciated the candor.

"Can you help her, Uncle Rhune? Will the Gift of Life enable her to settle down?" He lowered his voice and leaned close. "This can't be good for the baby."

"Yes, I believe I can help to an extent." He placed his finger on the clip of his cape, and it came away with a dot of blood on the tip. Touching it to Elaina's neck above the jugular vein, he closed his eyes.

Her lids flew wide with her gasp as a soft glow issued where his skin met hers. She gulped in air, threw her hands to her face, and then wrapped them around Rhune's arm.

Vincent scoffed his concern and looked at his uncle. "What's happening?"

"Firstly, I'm cleansing her blood of impurities not known of on Moraine. We can't have her passing on sickness they don't know how to deal with. Secondly, she'll need the immunities the average native would have to protect her from illness unknown to Terra. In short, my boy, I'm preparing her for life here."

Rhune gently wiped Elaina's brow. "Not to worry, my Terran butterfly. The discomfort will only last a moment. Once it passes, I'll present the Gift of Life." He smiled. "Which, by the way, has been described as one hell-of-a rush."

Rush or not, Vincent folded his arms, hoping it worked for Elaina's specific needs. As far as he knew, this had never happened before; a Terran bearing a Meridian child. For that matter, personally, he knew of no Meridians who had a child in their first lifespan. It was all so unbelievable.

He watched his love as her grip eased, and her jaw slacked. Small tremors shook her hands and legs, but the intensity seemed to have passed.

"Ah, now," said Rhune. "That's better. Now, let's get your system caught up with your new home."

New home. Did this mean she could never return to Cornerstone Deep? To her family? What was he thinking? Of course, she couldn't. *There's no way to return her before the rest of them follow, and then, the portal will be closed.*

Chapter Twenty-Eight

Cole leaned back in his chair as he watched the hologram over the Utopian mirrors. A sneer twitched his upper lip and forced his mouth into a deep frown. James saw fit to place a barrier over the portal right after the man jumped through. A bold call, to say the least. Then again, James' protective barriers left much to improve on compared to Cole's. They had four hours at most to complete all that needed to be done before the barriers faded and the ingrates began removing the ruble. Perhaps the noblemen would leave by then, realizing the task was fruitless.

He rolled his jaw and shifted his gaze to the side. Elaina had done the same as Lord Travis. Would she receive ill treatment? Though her desire was far from the nobleman's; that of praise to her chosen god and want for children. Perhaps her position in the Sentinel family gave her power in the form of favoritism? Whatever the case, he hoped she was safely on Midway Summit.

As he waved his hand at the door, it locked with a click. He did not need a disturbance during the final procedure, the procedure to call upon the Gods' powers to join theirs. For good measure, he added the silencing charm. *"Eko silyst.* I'm getting these globes ready without interruption this time."

Stepping to the three globes on the bookshelf, he closed the space with determination. Bitter knots clenched his stomach. *The final steps to prepare the globes for the sole purpose of closing the portal. Calm down Cole. If you prepare them wrong for the task...*

He didn't want to complete that thought.

He gathered the images in his mind, held his hands before him, palms outstretched. He spoke the final command. *"Optimal selentra!"*

The glow from the spheres increased. The light from each globe joined, washing out the color of the cherry-wood shelves. He placed his hand on Vincent's orb and called on the spell that would join the Gods' powers with it. *"Triad of Power, parclainum."*

The globe illuminated further, beams shooting through the space between his fingers. James' center sphere received the same gift. As he rested his hand on the third, a familiar tingle tickled his palm.

Cole caressed the smooth surface, allowing the warmth from within it to fill him. Closing his eyes, he opened his thoughts to cast the spell on his crystal.

A sharp knock came at the door.

Cole's lids flew wide, concentration shattered. *No!*

A loud pop filled the air, and a thin crack traveled the circumference of the magical sphere. Cole watched in horror as it split into a fork, and then again, until the body of the globe resembled crumpled leather. The light within died.

His gaze locked on the globe. Air refused to enter his lungs. Forcing his hands away from the dead orb, he raked his fingers across his scalp. He took a step back, and then another. He couldn't remove his gaze from the unmitigated destruction before him. Heart hammering, his cry muffled within the silencing spell.

"*No!*"

"Hey, man," came Jarrett's voice from the other side of the door. "I just wanted to..."

Cole's mind spun. He whirled around, thrusting his hand toward the locked door. Fire pellets bulleted the ingress, the force blowing it wide open with the stench of burnt wood.

Jarrett flew backward, tiny sparks bulleting his body. He landed on his butt with a heavy thud and barely caught himself from falling to his back. His eyes grew as round as saucers, but he finished his sentence anyway, all-be-it a whisper.

"...use your phone to call Mom and Dad before we leave."

Chapter Twenty-Nine

Cole glanced at Mianna as she placed clothes into a small duffle. Carriages clattered in his perception alongside the conversation she had in her head. How could she stand to have so much information from past lives always running through her mind? He grazed his chin with his nails and attempted to close off the communication coming into his thoughts. He had enough to worry about without more to press his anxiety further. How in the name of the Gods was he going to perform the Triad of Power without his globe? To be a conduit for the Gods' powers was unheard of, but it would be the only way to complete the task.

He lowered his gaze as a sick sensation sank in his stomach. He rubbed the spot. It wouldn't take his essence. That much he knew. The spell was completely different than the one his father had used. But to be a portal in his own right; a portal to the unharnessed power the globe should control... The task would be a dangerous undertaking. Yet it was the only one available.

Mianna's brows jumped, and she mumbled something as she reached for more items.

"My love," he said, in an attempt to break her concentration. "How many pieces of underclothes are you planning to bring? They do have such things we can purchase there."

She glanced at him, and then to her full hands. "Oh. Yes, well, I'm a bit pre-occupied. Did you know all creatures could be loyal to the point of death? I had no idea."

Huh. She garnered that from her conversation? "I can't say I did." He took the things from her grasp and returned them to the drawer. "Mianna, have I told you how relieved I am? How blessed I've become. When I was assigned to Midway Summit, all I could think was how I wouldn't have you there with me. We would spend an uncertain amount of years apart."

"The Gods wouldn't tie us together without preparing a way for us to accomplish our goal."

"I'm not speaking of a goal." He took her hands in his and closed the gap between them. "I'm speaking of the heart. I've spent the last four hundred years in loneliness, pining for your return even when I believed there would be no rebirth here for your soul. I couldn't bear a day of not knowing if I'd have you to share it with."

"Oh, my sweet led-by-the-heart man. I will always be by your side, touching your soul, if you but call to me." She gently removed her hand from his grasp and placed it against his cheek with a feather touch. A familiar verse dropped from her lips, sung with the most eerie, yet beautiful chord he'd heard.

"Call me with thine eyes, my love. May thy kiss be mine.
Fill my soul with Zephyr's breath, touch my heart so fine."

Contentment washed across Cole's shoulders and down his arms. Muscles melted as the long-forgotten language of his love lulled his heart. Mianna had been the only one to dilute him to the point of resembling a soggy rag, and he basked in the pleasure.

Her fingers combed through his long hair and rested at the back of his neck as she guided his lips to hers. Warm breath bathed his face as she sang.

"Bid the heavens part to us, send grace, light and fair.
Arylin, Goddess of Love, grant me now

my prayer."

Cole closed his eyes and leaned his head to brush his lips across her dainty wrist. The sweet scent of roses touched his senses.

"Sanction this, our unity, free from life's confines.
Love shall last o'er life's offing, eternally divine."

His lids fluttered open, and her brilliant gaze met his.

"Come with me my destiny, Free of all cares be.
See the love that harbors here, your serenity."

Skimming his hand around her slender waist, longing for her escape pooled deep. Would he survive sealing the portal with only two globes to aid in the process? Would he make it to Midway Summit to be at her side?
Time and questions ceased as she swayed, leading him into the center of their bedroom. Only Mianna existed. No portal. No doubt. He caressed her back, drawing tranquil circles on the fabric of her blouse.

The soft material offered reassurance of her gentle spirit and love. "My soul is yours, my love. My eternity is yours. Just say the word, and your will shall be done."

"As shall it be for you," she said with an airy breath.

Only everlasting love in the vastness of eternity surrounded them. Love, the way it was meant to be, was theirs now and forever.

Along with the myriad of conversations in her head. Would things ever be the same again?

A knot swelled in his chest as he knew the answer. "Mianna, my love, how do you do it? I know you're seeing more than what's happening between us right now."

Sparkles danced in her blue eyes, and she nodded. "So much knowledge is pouring through me, Cole." She motioned to take in the bedroom as a whole. "I see the wide fields of home. I see the geriatric ward I worked in as Airabelle. I hear the carriages of the eighteenth century." She brushed his lips with her fingertips and then dropped her voice to a whisper. "And then there's you."

He had hoped he would be in there somewhere.

She laid her head on the spot above his heart. "I feel your love so thick it's tangible.

It heats the blood in my veins and tastes like the richest nectar."

"Oh, my love..."

She placed her forefinger on his lips to hush him. "I knew you before. Did you know that?"

"Before what?"

"Before I was born I was granted a glimpse of my eternal companion. I knew you would find me, Cole. I knew as a child. I wrote that song when I was ten. I wrote it for you."

Chapter Thirty

As the back lawns of Shilo Manor came to view, reality flooded James' being, and he paused. It had been eight hundred years they'd spent on these grounds; eight hundred years of tears, joy, failures, and exaltations. So many beginnings, so many happenings.

He'd spent the evening with Sarah in the ornate belvedere, danced to the songs of blue jays and crows. Communed with the Gods in the topiary to his left, so many instances he'd forgotten the number, and refereed his brothers' arguments countless times within the walls of Shilo Manor. And he'd lost those he loved. How could he leave this haven of memories?

How could he not?

Solidifying his form on the backyard terrace, he looked at the statues that dotted the landing border. The crystalline within the rock sparkled, an obnoxiously charming sight in the light of the full moon. He averted his gaze, and it fell to the center of the landing beyond. He'd danced with Linda for the first time there, before getting interrupted by her father, and then had presented her with flowers from the edge of the topiary. He wiped his palm down his chest to settle the nostalgia and vowed to always hold the memories in his heart.

Linda and the twins sat quietly in the breakfast nook as James entered Shilo Manor through the back door. Mandy's foot tapped the leg of her chair while Mechenzie poked at the sandwich before her with her finger. One of Linda's hands clung to a mug of coffee while the other balanced a thin cigarette in her fingers. Smoke trailed into the magical conduit James had charmed the pack with, and he couldn't help grinning at the sight.

"You three are uncharacteristically quiet. Are things all right here?"

"We're going to miss Grand Momma and Grand Daddy," said Mandy, her little mouth barely moving.

Linda leaned her head to the side, and her blonde hair skimmed across her lovely shoulder. "I was just explaining that we wouldn't be coming back."

"I see."

"It's the only thing that has me worried about all of this now. I know as long as I'm with my girls, things will be fine with us. But what about Mom and Dad? They have nobody."

James lowered to one knee before her and lifted her hand from her cup. "Leenja, they have each other."

"But they *lived* for the times we were all together as a family, James. Dad being all huffy, and Mom fussing over us. And we aren't even able to say goodbye. Not properly. They both have important meetings today."

"No meeting is going to stand in the way of me seeing my daughters and grandbabies!"

James swiveled to look behind him as Linda's father stepped into the kitchen followed by her mother.

Linda sobbed a happy squeak, and James stood to allow her to go to them. She darted for their arms. "Mom, Daddy! Oh, how could you have known?"

Bethany fluttered her hand. "Oh, you can thank Jarrett for that. We'd just gotten back from our meetings when the phone rang. We rushed right over."

Ben huffed and tipped to his toes. "Seems the boy did something *right* after the mess he's made." He turned to James. "Now what's all this about you taking my *daughters* to live in some *other* dimension?"

"I'm afraid it's true, Ben. We've been reassigned to aid in the fulfilment of a prophecy. I'm sure I don't have to tell you how important such an assignment is."

Ben growled under his breath, and James knew the covenant of secrecy the family took part in at Vincent and Elaina's wedding would soften the stout man's regard. "Of course, you don't. But why take my daughters with you?"

James grimaced and set his hands at his waist. "Elaina has breached the portal and is already there on her own accord. She has selected a Goddess from that realm as her patron god, believing she would grant her the ability to bear a child. She wanted to be close to the Goddess Venus.

"Oh, my." Bethany flushed and clasped her hands. "Is that acceptable in the eyes of Arylin, Taravaughn, and Gryffin?"

"We've received no communication to the contrary, Bethany. And she's made her choice evident. And Linda insists on being with Mechenzie, who plays a vital role in the prophecy and must be trained there. We don't want to separate mother and daughter. I'm sure you understand."

Bethany covered her lips with her fingers. "So...they really are going to be gone from us." Tears brimmed her eyes. "And my baby is already gone. I can't even say goodbye."

Linda tilted her head, and her voice softened. "Oh, Momma, I'm sorry."

A muffled sob sounded in Bethany's throat. "Linda," she squeaked, and lunged for her arms again. Her shoulders shook as she wept. "I know the Founders work for the Gods. And...and I knew you two would be called on to work with them. But...all of you at once? To another *dimension*?"

Ben opened his arms, and the twins ran into his embrace. He cocked his head back and batted his beady eyes. "I'm going to miss you girls. I'm...I don't know...what we'll do without you two running around the house and leaving toys for me to step on in my bare feet."

Weak giggles muffled against his chest. "We'll miss you too, Grand Daddy," said Mandy.

"But we'll be back," added Mechenzie with a strained cheerful soprano. "Uncle Rhune will bless us, and we will be able to come back some day."

Though true, James tempered the desire to clarify and let the grandparents know many years may pass before that could happen. The next time they saw their loved ones, they could be well into adulthood.

Chapter Thirty-One

Elaina's eyes flashed with panic as Rhune took the place of midwife. Vincent's heart pounded against his Adam's apple and made it hard to swallow, but he forced the act to calm his nerves. How in the Spectrum of Realms had he come to the point of being a father? For that matter, how would he be a *decent* father? He was too carless, too selfish, and far too out of sorts to handle all this right now. But there he was, about to help Elaina deliver their baby. *Their* baby! *Gods, I need a drink...or...a tranquilizer!*

Scooting behind her on the bed, he pulled Elaina against him to help her recline. Her jittery hands flew to her face as Rhune lifted her skirt to her waist and prepared for the new arrival. "Wait! Vince, I changed my mind. I can't do this. I can't go through with it!"

Rhune chuckled, and his voice sounded far too calm for the situation. "My Terran butterfly, you'll do just fine. Motherhood is the most noble of callings and most natural of acts. What you must remember to do is breathe."

Vincent took a deep breath at the same time she did. They both nodded, and Vincent wrapped his arms around Elaina to hold her hands. Whether to show support, or out of desperation to control the moment, he didn't know.

"Good. Now focus on Vincent's hands to keep your mind steady. We don't need you to worry too much and destroy your health and that of the baby's, now do we?"

Vincent dropped his gaze to his hands and shook his head.

"Vincent, my boy, I was talking to Elaina."

Heat rushed his cheeks, but he didn't care much what Rhune thought of him at the moment. He might just go throw up. Or blow down the wall, whichever came to him first.

"You've done this before, right Uncle Rhune? I mean, this isn't the first—" Vincent swallowed the dryness in his throat. "—baby you've delivered."

The man had the nerve to chuckle again. "Who do you think delivered you? Your father was none too happy about it, but it couldn't be helped. He was out of reach at the time, and I was the only relative around. A trust such as this is kept within a Sentinel's family, you know."

"That's why you didn't take Elaina to a hospital? I thought it was so we wouldn't be seen."

"No, my boy. You will be seen by the natives soon enough. And a hospital isn't required." Rhune placed his hand above Elaina's large abdomen, and a soft glow issued from his palm. "The lad hasn't turned all he should," he murmured. Sliding his fingertips to Elaina's side, he smiled. "Ah, now that's better, isn't it?"

A huff came from Elaina's lips. "Is it? I feel like a basketball is pushing on my insides!"

"That would be the baby's head trying to poke out to see his lovely mother."

While Rhune seemed to be trying to lighten the moment, Vincent wanted to knock the block right off his uncle's shoulder. "Can't you do something to make her more comfortable?"

"Oh, my apologies, my Terran butterfly, are you hurting?"

Vince craned his neck to see her reaction.

She glanced to the side. "Well, no. Just the pressure, I guess."

Leave it to Uncle Rhune to have already thought of that and cast a spell to eliminate pain.

"And pressure is very good now as you must push."

Vincent's hands didn't veer from hers as she reached for her knees and grabbed them tight. A grunt gurgled in her throat as she bore down, and he unconsciously held his breath, applying pressure to his own abdomen. She released her breath with a heavy pant. Air rushed from his lungs.

"Again."

Vincent's growl rumbled alongside Elaina's cry as he strained at the same time she did. They leaned forward to press the effect further. Heat rose to his cheeks and tipped his ears, and his neck pulsed in a frantic rhythm to match the pounding in his head.

Elaina jarred with her gasp. Vincent sucked in air so fast he snorted. Heavy pants puffed beside his ear as Elaina rested her head back onto his shoulder.

"Get ready to give it another go," said Rhune with the most indecent cheerful voice a man could use. Didn't he know this was *exhausting* work?

Vincent looked at the man. "Already?"

"The head is out, my boy. We need one more shove and we'll have the little body."

Grasping Elaina's hands tighter, Vincent heaved a sigh. "Ready, Elaina? This is it!"

She rolled her head to the side and then nodded with a noisy swallow. They rocked to the count of three and then bore down to four, five, and six.

Tiny cries filled the room, and Elaina collapsed against Vincent's chest. "Tell me he's okay, Rhune. Please tell me!"

Vincent's gaze snapped to his uncle, and he didn't think he could wait for him to answer. But Rhune chuckled and stood with a pink bundle in his hands.

"*She* is very okay, my Terran butterfly."

Vincent's Adam's apple dropped to his heart, and he couldn't seem to get his throat to work. He forced a dry gulp as Rhune gently placed the baby in Elaina's arms and then wiped his hands on a towel.

Eternity expanded, sucking the air from the room, as Vincent wrapped his arms around Elaina and their baby. Could there be a more beautiful sight in the universe? He couldn't tear his gaze from the view over her shoulder. Hot tears brimmed his eyes and hazed his vision with mists of gray.

The ethereal plane had nothing to match the beauty that lay in Vincent's arms; Elaina and the most beautiful red-headed baby girl in the Spectrum of Realms.

Chapter Thirty-Two

Cole knew the moment James cast Shilo Manor into shadow. The study plunged into a dismal shade—the cherry desk and matching furnishings darkened, magical items that once gleamed went lack-luster. Light from the two remaining globes cast long phantoms behind the furniture, and the once beloved hallowed room seemed eerie.

The Memory Box and Moment Maker shot into his palms as he summoned them. Both of his father's prize relics had proven useful over the centuries—aside from the instance with Dressen—and he wasn't about to leave them behind for another set of Sentinels who had no idea how to use them.

He pressed his lips into a line and picked up the Candle Vignette. While a Utopian would be available at the Midway Summit Shilo Manor, Cole held tightly to the Shilo Family Candle Vignette. How priceless the images and information stored in it were to him. Joys and failures, losses and new beginnings, all told the story of their eight-hundred-year-stay in

Cornerstone Deep. And while he'd hated what seemed like much of it, the love he'd found could never be replaced. He wanted to savor the moments many more times. It slid easily into the large pocket inside his cloak.

Lifting from their plinths, the two crystal globes set the pace, and Cole marched down the hall to the foyer behind them. Their bright light washed the hazy walls to alabaster and cast shadows on the cherubim's profiles that lined the way. The fact his sphere couldn't join the others roiled in his gut. Gods be willing, two joining the Triad of Power would be sufficient to complete the procedure, and his task as the third conduit of energy would be light.

He teetered the Moment Maker in his left hand while he rested the rare Memory Box in his other cloak pocket.

As he entered the foyer, Mandy and Mechenzie dashed to James' side, packs bouncing on their backs. Each took hold of the fingers on his right hand. He slid the other around Linda's curvaceous waist and then looked at Cole. "Rhune isn't back to complete the Triad."

Cole heaved a sigh with his nod. "I thought of that. But we do have a Triad right here."

A furrow pressed down James' brows, and his gaze jumped to the little Meridian soul. "You can't be serious. Mechenzie?"

"It's the soul that holds the strength in a Triad, and hers is several lifetimes old. She's stronger than either of us."

James tried to step into a turn as he averted his gaze, but the girls stood in his way.

Linda leaned her head to look into her lover's eyes. "Is that true, James? Would she be strong enough to do it even if she's a child?"

Cole knew James couldn't deny it, as much as he might want to. With a hesitant nod, the Head of Sentinels consented. "It's against my better judgment, but technically, true."

"Then Mechenzie will take Vincent's globe when the time comes." Cole glanced at James and used his telepathic gift to quickly tell him what happened to his globe. "You'll take yours...and I'll stand in for mine."

James clenched his teeth and spoke to Cole's mind in a lowered voice. *"That globe was irreplaceable, Cole, but you even more so. I know there's no other way around this, but are you sure you can stand in as a conduit to the Gods' powers?"*

Mianna came to Cole's side with their

273

duffle, and he slung it to his shoulder. *"It's as you have said. There's no other way around this."*

As he took her in his embrace, Jarrett nodded his head of messy waves.

"Hey, thanks for letting me have some of Vincent's clothes. The guy has good taste." He flashed a smile and held out his palm. "Whose hand do I take?"

James' gaze snapped to him. "Who said *you* were going?"

"Uh." Jarrett tossed his hand toward Cole. "Mr. Sir Cole said if the Gods allowed it, I could." He took a step back as if to make sure he was out of James' striking distance. "You know, as the girls' father. They need their father. Dad said it himself."

Words punched into Cole's thoughts, and he cringed at James' mental shout. *"You told him he could come along? Now I'm drawing the line on you calling the shots! Everything passes by me first!"*

"There's a chance the gods will deny his entry, James," whispered Cole to his brother's mind. *"Just...have...faith."* He looked away at the weak comment. The chances were greater the gods would agree to the arrangement to allow the little family to stay together whether James liked it or not. A social divorce was between husband and wife, not father and children. James

274

would have a trying time ahead with Jarrett in the picture, but didn't they all?

James growled, and Cole cuffed at his cape, holding out the hem for Jarrett to take. "Hold onto this. You'll be fine."

"Oh, right. Hey, are we really going to fly like you guys do with that black smoke?"

"All the way there, Daddy," exclaimed Mandy. "Aren't we, Poppa James?"

"Yes, Mandy, all the way. And we had better get going."

As Jarrett opened his mouth to, no doubt, drop another "hey" beginning sentence, Cole shoved the cape hem into his hand and took on the Smoke of Night. James followed suit, and the globes trailed up the rear as the front door flew wide. Cole commanded the door to close and lock as they passed the threshold for the last time. He paused to view Shilo Manor in shadow, the first time in over eight hundred years he'd witnessed it. All the memories spent; the good and bad were locked away in the Candle Vignette and his memory. Would he ever see this place again in this lifetime? Perhaps, but be doubted Mianna would be with him.

How the Angel of Love would view this would be a mystery to unfold. Would Arylin visit her little sister there? Or would the sealed portal keep her firmly in her own domain? Regardless, he had Mianna, for more or for less, and he would revel in every moment they had together.

~ * ~

As they formed at the barrier before the granite bluff, their family group stood quiet. Cole picked up on a myriad of emotions: respect, fear, excitement, awe...

He scanned the area for a sign of the rogue noblemen, listening past their group's thoughts for any strangers' telepathic activity. His head bobbed with his leer. "They're out there watching us."

James heaved a sigh. "We can't have another barrier before the doorway while we seal it. It will interfere with the process."

"Then let the gods decide what to do with them if they attempt a breach."

Sucking in a deep breath, James lowered to one knee before Mechenzie. "What we are about to do will require all the magic you can give. Once we start, you must hold tightly to your Uncle Vincent's globe. Open your mind, try not to think anything, but let the power pour through you."

Mechenzie nodded and spoke with a strong little voice. "I understand. I won't let go until you do, Poppa James."

"Good girl."

Linda shuffled her feet in a nervous swagger. "This is safe, right? This won't hurt her, will it?"

James stood and placed his hand on her arm. "Leenja, she is a Meridian soul. It's what she's born to do. She's much stronger than you realize."

Cole didn't know when James had settled to that conclusion. Though true, instinct called to protect the young girl at all costs. This job was one meant for a grown Sentinel. But what choice did they have? It required a Triad of Purpose—three joining powers for one conclusion—having only two globes available would make it difficult to channel the strength of the Gods as it were.

Cole silently praised the fact it was his sphere that had burst. The oldest and most experienced should handle the task.

He scanned the faces of those under his care. "Once we get inside, James, Mechenzie and I will need to close the portal. But we can't have the rest of you there while we do it. It might take a while, and with your Terran origins, the nature of the gateway could cause problems for you. You'll need to go straight to Midway Summit. Keep it at the front of your thoughts and keep moving ahead. You'll get there."

Linda opened her mouth, but Cole held up his hand.

"You must believe in Mechenzie's own origin. She's Meridian in a Terran body. Her soul will protect her within the portal."

The mother's lips pressed together, and she blinked several times. A quick nod relayed her approval.

"Let's get this underway." Cole stepped to the face of the bluff and spoke in hushed tones as not to be heard by eavesdroppers. "Midway Summit."

As light overtook the arched doorway to the realms, James fisted his hands and then swept them to the side. The opalescent sheen of the protectant spell vanished, rubble tumbled from the portal, and Cole ushered his family through.

He tossed his gaze to the shadows. They were out there, and by the silence of their minds, he knew they attempted to hide their thoughts from him. But they couldn't hide their emotions. Their excitement and determination pounded against his senses. As he stepped into the portal, a mass of warped shadows surrounded them.

Linda quickly turned, her voice a mass of muffled words. "I changed my mind. I'm not stepping in another dimension without Mechenzie with me. I'm staying until you're done sealing the portal."

James shook his head. "No, Leenja. You must get Mandy to a safe place. I promise, I'll watch over Mechenzie."

Cole motioned to Jarrett with his nod and sent him a telepathic message. *"Here's your chance to play hero. Take the girls and get out. Just repeat Midway Summit and walk."*

Jarrett picked up Mandy, grabbed Linda's hand, and marched.

Linda's eyes flew wide, and her mouth dropped at the bold move. She quickly reached back, grasping Mianna's wrist.

Mianna's brows arched high on her forehead as she threw her gaze to Cole, eyes a mix of worry and well wishes.

In an instant, they were gone.

Shilo Manor series~Destiny

Chapter Thirty-Three

James took Mechenzie's small hands and placed them on Vincent's orb. "You hold the same powers as your Uncle Vincent does Kenzie. You will be able to control his globe. First, clear your mind."

She nodded and closed her eyes. "Okay, Poppa James."

The firmness in the tiny voice sent pride pulsing through James' heart. "Now concentrate on joining your powers with ours. Think of sharing all you have deep inside you with us."

The bright sphere lighted to the brilliance of high noon, and James squinted to control the intensity to his eyes.

"Very good. Now it's my turn. After I do the same, your Uncle Cole will do his part. Whatever you hear, or whatever you see, try not to be scared. He will take care of everything. Do you understand?"

She peeked between her lids, determination pinching her slight brows together. "Yes, Poppa James."

With a nod, James reached for his globe. He held it at arms' length, pointed at the portal door, and guided his energy to join with the Gods' power.

Cole held out both hands, palms forward, fingers splayed. He took a deep breath and uttered the first command. *"Partolca silyst."*

Arches flared from the globes and met with Cole's hands. His arms quaked as the raw energy poured through him, but he gnashed his teeth together and controlled the snarl playing on his lips.

James knew the absence of his globe would tax his brother, but he couldn't have imagined the impact the two globes at high potency would have on him. An orange glow surrounded the tips of his fingers, and the more James watched them, he realized the color wasn't from the power enveloping them, but pouring through them.

A thick mist spread from Cole's palms and covered the opening of the arch with an iridescent sheen. Pulses throbbed within the cover in an erratic rhythm, as if three heartbeats controlled a life therein.

Cole repositioned his stand, leaning into the magical charge. His lips dipped into a deep frown as his brows tightened.

Shouts came from the other side of the gateway, and James angled his head to see past the brightness. The form of a man appeared beyond the opalescent film. *Oh, don't be a fool. What is he doing?*

Undaunted by the intruder, Cole spoke the next command. *"Cartolca silyst."*

Silver sparks erupted from his hands, littered the barrier, and then thickened, overtaking the sheen with thick gloss.

Suddenly, the outline of a hand slammed against the silvery coating, and four clawed fingers reached within the portal pass.

Cole's ebony eyes glared at the man from the bottom of his furrowed brow. His deep sneer revealed the quiver in his chin.

"Back away," James growled.

An entire hand emerged, and Cole's arms flinched. He shook his head, squeezed his eyes shut, and barked the next two commands. *"Omereto silyst, arveta silyst!"*

A horrid scream sounded from the man on the other side as his arm crushed within the darkening sealant. Crimson liquid flowed in phantasmagoric shadows and seeped throughout the barrier like an untamed web. Red tinged the pulsating force, leaked into the thick power thread pouring from Cole's hands, and then stained the glow of his fingertips red. Tremors took his body, his cheeks quaked, and wrinkles formed within the deep furrows of his face.

James quickly glanced at Mechenzie, and then had to look again. Not only was she standing strong, eyes clamped shut, but her young body appeared to have grown by five, six years? She looked to be at least ten, and James couldn't believe what his eyes told him to be true. Could it be the portal's sporadic time equivalencies, or had he been concentrating on Cole's welfare so hard, he hadn't noticed the effect the process had on the little girl?

Cole heaved a breath and lowered his head, leaning further into the spell. His voice came forth forced. *"Miorta vi silyst, abigantra."*

Anxiety gnawed at James' gut. *This is too much for him. How could any man serve as a conduit for the power of the Gods? I should have had him wait for the new Sentinels to show before closing the portal.* He shook his head as the truth of the matter came to mind. *We had to act fast. There's no telling how long the Gods will deem this realm unsafe to host a gateway to the other realms.*

Cole sank to his knees, his elbows bent as if he held the weight of the world. James quickly stepped beside him and hooked his arm under his brother's for support. Mechenzie did the same, and James' jaw dropped.

She looked like a young woman, tall and strong willed. As her gray eyes met his gaze, she nodded, and he knew she understood. Things would never be the same. While she grew, Cole's countenance faded. From youth to aged, his hair lightened, skin withered, face displayed the unshaven years of struggle with the Gods' power.

James resisted the urge to check his own chin for signs of growth, though he knew what the prickle had meant when he felt it a moment ago.

Brilliant power flowed from the globes, to Cole's hands, and then pulsed toward the gateway, creating a solid barrier, discolored by the blood of the trapped limb.

Cole's head hung forward, and his weight increased on James' arm. White strands formed within his long crown of hair, and as James looked at Cole more fully, he noticed facial hair growing by inches. Time was passing too quickly. *We've got to get this port sealed!*

As if Cole had read his mind, he spoke the final command with a crackle in his voice. *"Partolca silyst. Vi omicorto silyst!"*

The barrier turned gray, the globes' lights faded, and James felt Cole's shudder hit his orb.

~ * ~

Cole's knees weakened and threatened to give way. Surrealism surrounded him in a haze of warped shadow and waves of nausea. He quickly sent a mental command to the Candle Vignette in his pocket. *"Chronicles of Shilo Manor, entry, My love, Mianna."*

Using his telepathic gift, he spoke to the record keeper.

"They say love will always find a way, it's always darkest before the dawn, we must go through the bad to appreciate the good, every storm cloud has a silver lining, and we all have the potential to one day be as the Gods. But all of these have one thing in common; for them to mean anything to us, we must have the insight to see the big picture.

"My whole life, I've tried to keep this in mind, to see things in an eternal perspective, and have failed miserably. Perhaps it was wired into my psyche at birth as a trial to overcome, or my own shortsighted goals that would only afford me to see the present. Regardless, I've always been nothing without you, my love. The heavens could open and pour blessing upon me beyond dreams, and I would see nothing without your eyes, feel nothing without your heart, and understand nothing without your soul there to show them to me. Colhart Nixtoro

Krylu Shilomacj. The greatness in the names is lost to me without you. Emptiness engulfs me in the moment, expands to stretch out on every side, when you're not there."

Cole lowered his head, and the weight of the power caused his arms to weaken.

Complete the task. A conduit, he must relay the power of the Gods.

James hooked his arm under Cole's elbow and then Mechenzie did the same. Relief washed through his exhausted muscles, and he focused on his discourse to his love between channeling the energy and fighting to stay upright.

"My mind grows weak. My body fatigued... My eyes are heavy. I fight to keep focused. Oh, that I could blink, and this bitter end be gone. For I feel...this is the end, my love."

He shuddered as tremors took his body.

Breathe.

He needed to breathe.

"My vision is... darkening. Shadows of... doubt... overwhelming."

Fear.

"Will I see you again, my love, in this life time? Oh, that I could awake and... find you watching me... across... a bay of never ending time... where none... depart. Where love..."

Chapter Thirty-Four

James released his globe as Cole crumpled to his knees, and then to the side. He quickly lifted his brother into his arms and motioned to the young woman standing beside them. "Mechenzie, grab my sphere and take hold of my cape. Don't let go."

She wrapped her arm around the balls and then grasped his cloak tightly with her free hand. Her blonde brows pressed into a high arch, determination replaced by fear in her bright gray eyes. A quick nod told him she was ready.

"Midway Summit." James marched ahead.

A tall doorway appeared before them and, as they stepped across the threshold, the wide view of a waterfall filled the space. Splashes filled the air, mineral water assaulted his nasal cavities, and his shoes skidded on the slick rock.

James laid Cole on the wet ground at his feet.

As the portal closed, he rummaged through Cole's cape for the Moment Maker. "Cole needs immediate attention. We're going to travel fast." He found what he sought, and quickly dialed the circular base of the spindle. "This will give us a small amount of time in our favor, but I'll need you to fly as fast as you can so my energies can focus on carrying Cole. He can't be within the magical time period. His timing needs to stand still with the rest of the world, or we could lose our chance of getting him the help he needs before it's too late."

"I'll fly fast, Poppa James."

Her voice sounded foreign, and James unconsciously glanced at her to marvel at the phenomenon. The six-year-old little girl he knew her to be stood before him fully matured into a young woman. Long blonde hair reached to her thighs and framed her angular face with long waves. The chipmunk cheeks he'd loved had disappeared to cover a dainty jawline and meet a narrow nose. Her thin lips twitched, as if her tone had surprised her too.

Shaking himself back to reality, he blinked. *Stay focused!*

He took her hand and spoke the command to the Moment Maker. "*Mirhus silyst.*"

A wave of nausea washed over him with a heavy metallic scent, and he glanced at Mechenzie as she placed her hand on her stomach. He should have warned her of the discomfort, but after what they'd just experienced this was nothing, and time was of the essence.

Motion ceased. Water hung before them in frozen flows. Droplets in mid-descent stood before them like a halted hologram.

James swiped aside the miniscule sprays that had rebounded from the rock. They floated to the far side of the concave. Stooping to pick up Cole, he carefully lifted him into his large arms, and then dispersed his lower body into the Smoke of Night. Mechenzie dissolved, and James felt her presence holding tightly to his. He shot through the small space between the water fall and mountainside, knocking droplets aside from their halted downward course.

Stillness painted the countryside on a vivid backdrop of a multitude of color. From deep green to bright purple, foliage covered the mountain and surrounding fields. A light blue sky hosted the white sun in full array. Warmth kissed his cheeks as it seeped through his skin to his bones for the first time, it seemed, since he'd gone to the frigid temperatures of Cornerstone Deep. How he missed the Meridian sun and the constant heat.

He allowed the warmth of this realm to fuel his flight, relishing it as it reminded him of his home. Feeding his will, he pushed his half-phased body into an outright sprint. Mechenzie's particles thinned, and he made a conscious effort to cling tighter to her as not to lose her.

James glanced at Cole as he lay stiffly in his arms, and anxiety knotted his chest. The white sun erased the shadows from his face and washed his skin to a sickening pale. His gaze flew over the platinum hair of Cole's face and head, and then to the darkened skin on his brother's hands and arms.

To use a conduit of the Gods' powers was one thing, but to be that conduit was a completely different matter. Would his heart, his mind, be the same? He couldn't imagine the toll it had taken on his brother. Would he make it in time to save his life, much less his health?

An enormous city expanded ahead of him, and James unconsciously paused to take it all in. Traffic stood motionless along wide byways around the city, lanes of floating vehicles a Midway realm should have never imagined. Skyscrapers reached upward. Sunbursts gleamed off mirrored buildings, and he searched for a reason this dimension could have advanced to such lengths before a cornerstone realm had.

Mechenzie's quizzical thoughts hit him, jarring him back to his task.

He swooped to the left to follow the base of the mountain to where Shilo Manor had stood so many years before. The stately home appeared around a rolling mound, surrounded by acres of white-capped orchards.

Knowing the front door wouldn't respond to a command given under the Moment Maker's control, James pulled his essence together on the front porch.

Mechenzie formed beside him, panting. "Poppa James, I'm sorry. I tried to keep up the best I could."

"You did very well, Kenzie, but right now, we need help." He quickly nulled the moment with his command. *"Conmirhus silyst."*

The world turned into a myriad of noises: birds, bugs, traffic, the breeze through the trees...

The front door flew open, and before James could take in the scene, Rhune took Cole from his arms and placed him on the veranda floor. He removed a knife from his jacket pocket, opened it, and then sliced into his own palm. Without a flinch, he threw his hand to Cole's neck. Rhune's nostrils flared as a heavy glow issued from where skin met skin. "Come on, Colhart. I refuse to let you die!"

Wind whipped, white petals tumbling

over the landing in a fury, and James uttered a silent prayer. *"Please don't take him due to his heroism."*

Cole jarred, a deep gasp shuddering his cheeks. His eyes peeled open, and for the first time, James saw the extent of agony the ethereal act had on his brother. White shadows clouded the onyx irises. Deep wrinkles edged the corners of his eyes, and if James hadn't known better, he'd swear he stared at a ghost.

"Thank the Gods." Rhune removed his blood-soaked hand and gathered Cole into his arms. "Let's get him inside quickly."

James held the door as Rhune sidled inside and headed for the parlor. "How did you know to be right here when we released the Moment? You were right at the door."

"Son, I've had an alert on the scry for activity of the portal for ten years now."

"Ten years! That much time has passed?" He looked at Mechenzie, whose eyes glistened with moisture. She bit her lower lip, and a sob shook her shoulders. All those years, her childhood had disappeared. A span of time she could never relive or get back.

But instead of the shed tears for herself, her whisper revealed her true concern. "Momma must have been sick with worry that whole time."

"Right you are, my special dove. For the first three years, she insisted on me and Vincent flying her there to stay through the day. Your father took her place at night." He looked at her and nodded. "He's been mighty worried too."

"Daddy did that?"

"Your aunt Mianna helped out at times, and Elaina wanted to join them too, but with the baby and all, it made it difficult to spare the time."

Mechenzie voiced James' astonishment at the same time he did. "Baby?"

"Oh yes. Lacey is a fiery little girl, if you catch my drift."

Cole groaned as Rhune rested him on the cushions of a leather sofa. In his weakened state, his head lolled to the side and his hand slid to the floor. Rhune gently place it on his waist and tucked a pillow beneath his neck.

"I don't know what you all have been through in that portal. But I'm inclined to believe the worst. And for Colhart to attain such a state, it had to do with channeling the ethereal."

"His globe was damaged. He used himself as a conduit."

Rhune nodded. "Then, while the results of the stress may be permanent, the gods are likely to grant that he lives after my Gift of Life administration."

Mechenzie seemed unable to speak above a soft chord. "Where is everybody?"

"In the back. It's Lacey's birthday. Mandy prepared a special celebration. But I think we should get Colhart squared away here before we spring this development at them. And you, young lady, had better go up to your sister's room and change into something that fits you properly. We don't need you parading around here in a skirt that barely covers your...uh... You catch my drift."

Mechenzie looked to her short skirt and tight blouse that barely covered her breasts and blushed. She quickly folded her arms around her chest, and her lower lip pouched out into a pout. "Okay," she said in a tiny voice. "Do we have the same room?"

With a grin, Rhune nodded. "And same bedspread. She refused to get a new one until you were here to pick it out together."

"Oh, Mandy..." Tears fell to her cheeks. "Does she have big," she glanced at her bosoms and turned bright red. "Poppa James," she squeaked.

James leaned his head to the side and picked up a throw from the back of a chair. Placing it on her shoulders to give added coverage, he wrapped his arms around her.

"It's okay, Kenzie. We'll get through these changes. And I'll bet Mandy will be your biggest supporter."

Her sob punched the air as she rushed off.

Rhune passed his hand over Cole's eyes. "Do you see at all, Colhart?"

Cole's voice rasped, and it sounded painful to speak. "I see shadows. Where's Mianna?"

"She's with the others, my boy. Let's get your sight and strength back, and then I'll call her to you." He placed his blood-stained palm over Cole's brow and in a low tenor commanded the healing energies of his Gift of Life. "*Brayton ambrelo. Amorianta.*"

A deep breath shook Cole's shoulders as his chest expanded. His mouth dropped open, as a stifling groan gurgled in his throat. He flexed his fists, bent his knees, and seemed to try to double into himself.

Rhune placed his other hand on Cole's chest. "Try to relax, my boy. You've aged considerably due to the stress put on your body. There will be many changes you'll have to consider now."

As Rhune removed his hand from Cole's brow, his lids blinked wide. The off-white clouds that covered his irises faded to a dull gray.

"Somebody turn on the lights," grumbled Cole. "It's too dark in here."

"Ah, well, the lights are on." The tone in Rhune's voice couldn't have been graver. "Shadows cover your sight. It could get better with time, but not by much, I'm afraid. Age is nothing anyone can reverse."

James lowered his gaze. Such a sacrifice Cole had made to ensure a complete sealing of Cornerstone Deep's gateway to the realms, an act worthy of more than an aged body. But then again— he looked at Rhune—if it hadn't been for his uncle...his father...it would have been his life Cole had sacrificed for the cause.

Chapter Thirty-Five

Cole stroked his white beard, marveling at the length it had grown in the short time they'd fought with the closure of the doorway to the realms. He slowly rose from the sofa and then shuffled to the wide mirror on the east wall of the parlor. His long hair seemed to be at least two feet longer, and the lack of pigment cast a white glow to his crown.

The glass reflected the large room with one dominant item missing. His father's portrait. How many years had he sat across from the depiction and spoke as if the man stood there ready to give advice? With the happenings of the last several months, he would never want for advice from the Senior Sentinel again.

He ran his palm down his beard again and then gingerly touched the deep wrinkles that creased his face. What was ten years in Midway Summit equivalent to in Meridian time? No doubt the process affected him in ways he didn't understand while in the place that had no understanding of time. He'd worked directly with the Gods on this matter.

Perhaps it *had* grabbed the Meridian timeline to add to the taxation of his system. He quickly figured a loose translation of the math. *I'd be...eight thousand twenty-five by Meridian...seventy-three by Midway? And I left Cornerstone Deep a healthy thirty-two.*

He groaned. *I feel ten thousand ninety-two.*

But what of Mianna? She had turned twenty-five not long before he'd harvested her for Lord Dressen that fated night. She was now thirty-five and married to an ancient. How could she love him in such a state?

"Cole? Cole!"

His heart turned to butter as he heard his love's anxious voice from the receiving hall. As much as he wanted to rush into her arms, insecurity kept him rooted to the spot. Mianna's reflection appeared around the corner, and he glanced away, as if it would hide his appearance.

"Oh, sweet Arylin, Cole," she cried as she dove for him. "I've prayed every hour for your return to me since we came to Moraine. We waited all day for you to follow us, and then watched the Utopian for a sign of you all night. You didn't come out. I feared the worse! But every scry Rhune performed stated that you were

Charlene A. Wilson

untraceable. He assured us that meant you were still alive, just not on this plane."

"Oh, my love. I was very much alive, and I prayed for our reunion unceasingly."

"But you've been hurt badly." She brushed the white hair from his face and gazed adoringly into his eyes. "Are you well?"

Cole smiled. How could she look at him with such love in her gaze, with such adoration in her emotions? He felt the creases in his eyes deepen with his smile. The love pouring from her soul seemed to have doubled from the last time he'd seen her. Or was it the fact they had thought they'd lost each other that compounded the cherishment?

"I'm well; though I have aged I'm afraid. As you can see, I no longer appear in my thirties."

Laughter punched from her lips, and it was the most beautiful sound he'd ever heard. "Oh, Cole, you look perfect." She laid her head on his chest as she wrapped him in her embrace. "So perfect. Wasn't it you who has always reassured me that the soul will never age? Only grow in spirit and knowledge. And you..." Her gaze met his again. "You and I will be together so much longer than these mortal bodies will."

"Oh, but my love..."

She looked deep into his eyes, and he saw eternity in the sparkle of her blue irises. "What is it you told me when my life was nearing an end as Mianna, Cole?"

He leaned is head, love coursing through every vein in his wrinkled body. "Though eyes may dim and the body fades, love grows in an eternal realm of ageless spirits. Flesh cannot take away that which our souls have united. My love, my eternity is yours." Cole's heart wrapped around the reality—forever and always, he and Mianna, whatever lifetime they lived in, would be together.

"And my eternity is yours, my sweet Cole."

Warmth wrapped them in a thick mist, and he knew it was true. Heaven deemed it so, the Gods anointed their love, and no matter the course they must take, their destinies were united as one.

~ * ~

Laughter filtered through the back door from the kitchen, as Linda's alto could be heard over bickering young voices. James smiled and glanced at Mechenzie.

She threw him a grin and scrunched her nose. "Sounds just like Momma. She's always trying to keep me and Mandy from fighting." She sniggered, and her gaze lowered, taking in her body. "Do you think they'll know me, Poppa James? I feel like I don't even know me."

"They'll know who you are Kenzie, not to worry."

Rhune paused beside the breakfast nook and folded his arms over his chest. "You're holding up well, my little dove. Do you feel weak or faint?"

Mechenzie shrugged, and her long hair fell from her shoulders. "I think I'm okay, Uncle Rhune. Just a little tired."

He nodded. "Well, I'm here to assist with the Gift of Life if your Terran body fails you."

James scrubbed at his beard and then raked his fingers over his scalp. His hair had grown to lengths he never thought he'd allow, but he wasn't going to take the time needed to shave and trim. Linda could choose which way she preferred him, and he'd adjust it to her liking.

He silently thanked the Gods his body only aged the ten years they appeared to have missed, and not been dealt the cards Cole would live with. A twinge of guilt rushed to his cheeks, but it fled as he thought about Linda. He wanted to hold her, feel her soft body wrapped in his firm biceps as she leaned into him. The planes of his chest ached to savor her bosoms press against them, and his hands longed to explore the dip of her waist as it made way for her voluptuous hips. "I think we'd both just like to see everybody, Rhune."

With a nod, Rhune took a step. His shoulders filled the doorframe from jamb to jamb. "My dear family. I believe I have news that will make this day even brighter."

"For my birthday, Uncle Rhune?"

James didn't recognize the little quizzical voice.

"For all of us, on your special birthday, my little Lacey doll." He stepped onto the terrace landing and turned, looking at James and Mechenzie.

Mechenzie took a little step back. "I'm scared. What if they don't like how I look? Or that I'm not really sixteen, Poppa James. I just turned six! What do I do?"

James took her hand and gave it a little squeeze. "They'll love you all the same, Kenzie. Come on, we'll go together."

"Okay, but you first."

He pressed his lips into an understanding grin and walked to face those he loved most. A young girl with fiery red hair hopped onto Vincent's lap as he sat in a lounge beside the picnic table. Elaina poured colorful liquid into cups, while Linda sliced cake and then placed it onto a plate. Mandy, the identical image of her sister, noticed him first.

Her eyes grew wide. "Pa... Poppa James?"

James' grin grew to a wide smile, and his dimples pressed into his cheeks. "And I'm not alone."

Mechenzie stepped to his side. "Hi, Mandy."

"Oh, dear Gods! Momma, it's Kenzie!" Her short hair, feathered with colors of pink and blue, fluttered in the wind as she ran to her twin and then threw her arms around her.

Linda dropped the knife from her hand and ran so hard her bosoms bobbed with each lunge. "James! Mechenzie! Oh, dear Arylin, oh, gracious Taravaughn, dear, merciful Gryffin!" She threw a chair from her path. "Get out of my way." The girls' little huddle turned into an eight-arm struggle to hug tight enough as James and Linda embraced with the twins in the middle.

Jarrett rushed from the side line and seemed unable to find a place to join in the hug. "Kenzie Pop, my golden girl number two! Hey, it's Daddy. Boy, have we missed you!"

A hammer drummed James' heart as the man's excitement forced reality into the equation. Jarrett had just spent ten years with Linda, and James hadn't been around to witness all that had happened. *Gods, nothing better have happened!*

He scowled at the man, but it didn't seem to deter the fool's enthusiasm. Pure joy lit every part of his scrawny body as he hopped around the tight circle as if to say, *let me in too!*

James refused to accommodate him and leaned his cheek on Linda's sweet hair. Hot mist manifested under his lids and stung his eyes. He blinked hard to release the tears and allowed the moment to wash over him.

Rhune laughed, his arms bobbing on his chest, as Vincent and Elaina rushed over to join in the circle.

"Lacey, this is your Uncle James and Cousin Mechenzie," announced Vincent. "Gods are we glad to see you! But where's Cole? He's with you, isn't he?"

James straightened and looked him in the eyes. "Yes, he's here. But there's something you should know before you see him."

"Wait. He's okay, isn't he?"

A tired voice came from the door. "He's just fine. Just a little...old."

As Cole and Mianna walked around the group, Jarrett halted his antics and stared at Cole. "Holy skylark. Hey, talk about the spitting image of a wizard!"

Chapter Thirty-Six

Linda, Jarrett, and Mandy seemed unable to tear their gazes from Mechenzie as they stood beside the hearth of the study. How the girl would manage to mature quickly enough to catch up to her body, Cole didn't know. She displayed a personality advanced for her six-year-old self in the past, perhaps her soul's experiences would aid in the process.

Vincent balanced Lacey on his knee, while Elaina held her hand at his side. The peculiar phenomenon definitely ranked up there with extraordinary blessings to Shilo Manor, but he believed, while Mandy and Mechenzie seemed mild and preoccupied with each other at play, this young one would be a handful. A chuckle played in his heart. *I bet Kid is getting his payback for his youthful stunts.* With humor in his foresight, he imagined many more outbursts between him and Vincent over the matter.

A child. He shook his head, and his heart melted. *A true blessing to the Shilomacj family.*

James took his place in the master chair. Linda obviously preferred her men clean shaven as he'd returned to his trimmed, neatly presentable self in a matter of hours.

Rhune leaned on the door jamb in a very Vincent-like manner.

Mianna closed the door, and then joined him beside the wide tapestries along the east wall. Her arm wrapped around his waist as her hand settled atop his long beard. Cole smiled. Mianna seemed to have found the whole aging process amazing and couldn't manage to keep her hands off the thing. So be it, if it made her happy. He'd play the wise old coot.

He glanced at the beautiful renditions of Meridian beside them, his home realm: the five moons, indigo sun, white fields, and the Arched Spectrum of Realms. Never again would he feel nostalgic over the place. His home was now here with Mianna, and a house full of lovingly irritating bustle.

James issued the essential command. "*Eko silyst.*"

As he passed his hand over the family's Candle Vignette, a wide flame flickered to life. He looked at each family member in turn, and Cole followed his regard. He loved them, cherished them, and would want to spend the rest of his life with no other group of people.

James' gaze fell on Rhune, and Cole

widened his perception to read the emotions emitted. If he read James right—and he knew he did—tenderness had replaced all anger at the man. His thoughts came to Cole clearly, but he wasn't who needed to hear them. "James, is there something you'd like to say before we begin?"

"Yes." Lacing his fingers in front of him, James seemed to consider his words. "We've all been through a lot. We've lost, we've discovered things about ourselves, and we've deepened our love. By the grace of the Gods, we've made it to this moment. But by the care of one man, we've been able to stay close and continue our lives together." He looked at his father, and his lips teetered as she spoke. "Rhune, you've watched over our loved ones, protected them when we weren't here to do so. You've shared the Gift of Life. You've...become invaluable to the family."

Rhune lowered his gaze and smiled. "Thank you, son."

"But I will never be able to call you father." James chuckled. "No matter how many times you call me son...or rainbow flower...or whatever other name you come up with."

A chorus of laughter sprang in muffled tones within the silencing spell of the room.

James nodded toward Rhune. "No offense."

"None taken, son."

"So, back to the reason we're here." He looked at the Candle Vignette. "The Chronicles of Shilo Manor."

The heading appeared within the flame as James dictated, and reverence replaced the cheer in the hallowed study. "A new era has begun. Enter... Midway Summit."

End Book Three

Please continue
to enjoy a special Bonus Chapter
written especially for Shilo Manor
fans!

DESTINY

Chapter Thirty-Three

Bonus Chapter

Mechenzie

Mechenzie watched as Daddy disappeared into the empty white of the portal with Momma and Mandy. Nerves in her tummy didn't just flip-flop, they skipped rope! As much as she wanted to help Poppa James and Uncle Cole, she couldn't keep her insides from shaking. Did destiny really want her to be as good as the grown-ups? How in the world could she do *that*?

She looked at the floor, insecurity throwing all the reasons it couldn't work through her mind. Her eyes grew wide. No floor. *No floor!* Tossing her arms out to her sides for balance, she gasped. *How can I be standing on nothing?*

Poppa James' large hands folded over hers. Guiding her to Uncle Vincent's floating orb, he placed them on either side and then looked deep into her eyes. So many of his hopes and plans for her echoed from his heart to hers. He believed in her, in her ability to do what needed to be done. She forced all her attention on him. If he believed, she would too.

"You hold the same powers as your Uncle Vincent does, Kenzie. You will be able to control his globe." He took a deep breath, and she did too, determined to follow his example to the T. "First, clear your mind."

As much as she hated to look away from him, she closed her eyes and then nodded. "Okay, Poppa James."

"Now, concentrate on joining your powers with ours. Think of sharing all you have deep inside you with us."

But... how? How could she share powers? She couldn't just break it in half like a candy bar and give them a piece.

As if he'd heard her, Uncle Cole's voice entered her mind, clear and strong. *"It's like sharing love, Mechenzie. It comes from your... heart. Like when you give a hug. Let it flow through your chest, down your arms, and into the globe like you're holding our hands."*

Eager to try this new idea, Kenzie thought of the love she felt. She imagined Mandy, Momma, Aunt Elaina, and her newly found family with the Shilos. In an instant, an invisible door deep inside flew open. Heat poured forth, swirled around her heart, divided to fill both arms, and then spread through her hands like fire down each finger. Sharp tingles prickle her palms and laughter bubbled in her throat. She bit her lips together to make sure she didn't giggle.

"Very good," said Poppa James. "Now it's my turn. After I do the same, your Uncle Cole will do his part. Whatever you hear, or whatever you see, try not to be scared. He will take care of everything. Do you understand?"

She peeked between her lids. "Yes, Poppa James."

With a nod, he reached for his globe, held it at arms' length, and pointed at the portal door. In a flash, his glowing, white ball burst so bright she pinched her eyes shut to stop the sting it caused.

Kenzie forced her thoughts to open the door deep inside her wider and let the warmth flow. *Share the love. Share my power.*

Streams of heat grew to sparkling rivers that filled every bit of her body. Her feet itched, muscles in her legs twitched, and spirals of energy circled up her spine to her head. Uncle Cole's voice punched through the wild sound of waves in her ears.

"Partolca silyst."

Kenzie's ball jarred, and she flinched, eyes flying wide. Bright silver arches pierced the blinding light from the orbs and then met with Uncle Cole's hands. His arms shook, and he gnashed his teeth together with a frightening snarl. An orange glow surrounded the tips of his fingers.

Squinting, she watched through the tiny slits between her lids.

A thick mist spread from his palms and covered the portal door with a silky cover.

Uncle Cole shuffled his feet and leaned into the flow of magic. His lips dipped into a deep frown as his brows tightened.

Shouts came from the other side of the gateway, and Kenzie shifted her eyes to try to see what was happening. A shadow appeared beyond the film, but Uncle Cole spoke again.

"*Cartolca silyst.*"

Sparks poured from his hands, sprinkled over the barrier, and then the film look like a heavy glass.

Suddenly, the outline of a hand slammed against the silvery coating, and four clawed fingers reached within the portal pass.

Kenzie gasped, closed her eyes tight, and focus all her strength. *Power, reach the crystal ball in my hands.*

Poppa James shouted something, but she ignored him, just as he had told her. *"Whatever you hear, or whatever you see, try not to be scared."*

"Uncle Cole will take care of everything," she whispered, but the soft words drowned as surges punched through her heart. Heat burned her cheeks and gushed down her arms. Tiny hairs stood on edge as it pulsed under her skin. Tidal waves roared in her head until her ears muffled and could hear nothing but her fast heartbeat and breathing.

Silver and sky-blue streamers grew within the spiral of fine mist rushing before her mind. Kenzie floated with the breeze-like motion, accepted it, welcomed it. This was her power, her moment, and there would be no hiding this time, no shame.

Calm encircled her as she allowed it to take control. Faces formed, and she watched as memories of each filled her. Yes, these were memories! With every pass, another story unfolded. So quickly, and too many to count, Kenzie soaked up every heartfelt one without care to reason. It all felt so right.

Times, experiences, lives, stacked upon each other until knowledge filled her so fully she needed breath for relief. She inhaled, and sugar air tickled her nostrils. The portal. They were in the portal, closing the gateway to Cornerstone Deep... her home. But not really her home. Her soul belonged elsewhere. Yes, that was what it was called, that part of her so deep she could taste forever... eternity. Every misfortune, every exhalation, from her home in that foreign dimension filled her. So many she didn't think her body could hold them, she accepted. She knew them, had loved them.

In a distant thought, Uncle Cole's voice rode the torrent. *No, not Uncle.* Her eyes burned as mist forced its way under her lids, and the truth bit reality into her understanding. *Oh, Colhart.*

Look for more of the
Shilos in book four
Awaken

Also, check out Aumelan, *Blessed of the Gods*, and see a whole new side of Moraine, Midway Summit!

Arched Spectrum of Realms

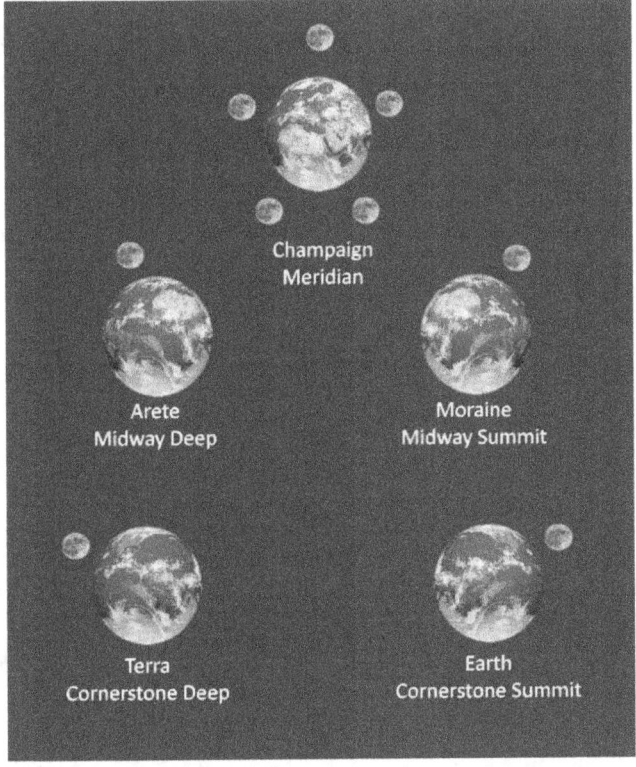

"This is Meridian, my home. It's the oldest dimension in the Arched Spectrum of Realms. You might call it the mother of the planes. She's the original that all others are patterned after."

—*Vincent, Fated*

Get your own printable
Vignette Journal
FREE!

When you join Charlene's VIP Readers mailing list, you'll get behind-the-scenes info on all her books, be the first to know when new releases become available and have a chance to be part of her exclusive teams! And of course, you'll get a special Printable PDF—designed so you can staple or add holes to put in a favorite binder—so you can create your own Vignette Journal and record those magical moments to relive any time you wish.

Get it NOW at: CharleneAWilson.com!

Please Consider Leaving a Review

Share your experience of *Destiny* with others! Honest reviews help readers find books they will enjoy, and it helps authors with visibility and rank. Just write a few (or more!) thoughts you have about this book at [Amazon](#) or [Goodreads](#). Your help will make a big difference, and I would really appreciate the time you take with this!

About the Author

Charlene A. Wilson is a USA Today Bestseller who writes stories that take you to other dimensions. She weaves magic, lasting love, and intrigue to immerse you into the lives of her characters.

She is the mother of two beautiful children and resides in a small community in Arkansas, USA, with her husband, a shy Pekingese, and a very chatty cockatiel named Todder.

Author site:
http://CharleneAWilson.com
Facebook:
http://facebook.com/CharleneAWilsonFan
Twitter:
http://twitter.com/AuthorCAWilson
Instagram:
http://instagram.com/CharleneAWilson
Pinterest:
http://pinterest.com/CharleneAWilson

Charlene A. Wilson

Also by
CHARLENE A. WILSON

Her Shadow Demon

Shilo Manor Series
Fated
Echoes
Destiny
Vignette Journal (Cornerstone Deep
version)
Awaken
Coming Soon
Chosen

Aumelan Series
Blessed of the Gods
Coming Soon!
World Beneath the Rock